# GARGANTUAN
## A Deep Sea Battle

Alan Spencer

# PART ONE: COAST ATTACK

# On the Boardwalk

Five o'clock on a California summer afternoon, you bet the Santa Cruz beach boardwalk was busy with tourists. The boardwalk bustled with citizens enjoying the classic amusement park rides, like the Giant Dipper, Cyclone, Logger's Revenge, and Double Shot. Across from the vintage rides, the beachgoers were trying to catch what was left of today's sunshine.

What they would also catch was death.

Surging from the Pacific Ocean, the two-ton creature displaced enough water to cause a rolling tsunami wave to smash into the boardwalk. Rides were shattered into high-flying tatters by the force of the enormous wave. Helpless citizens were sucked under the water's wicked power. Those who were far away enough from the shoreline were screaming and running for their life. Barbara Hampton, who had been about to relax on the beach, called the police on her cell phone. Barbara was screaming for the authorities to send help, and send it now.

*What can the police do about this*, Barbara thought, even as she heard the dispatcher talking on the other end. Every ounce of gall drained from her body once she saw the beast surface from the ocean. The eye really had to take in the enormity for several seconds before recognition of any kind could be made. This was like no beast she had ever seen before. The thing was spinning like a thrown disc and traveling high up in the air. The chopping sounds were deafening as it kept taking flight. There was only one thing she could compare it to, and that was a giant starfish. The five prongs were made of thick bone and caked in an ancient greenish-black algae. The rest of its mass was a drab gray color. Each prong was slashing through the air, slicing through the tops of skyscrapers, tearing highways into pieces, and colliding into cars and downgrading them into steel pulp.

Ten city miles were turned inside out in less than fifteen minutes. Flames were breaking out in pockets of the city and spreading in residential and business districts. Fire trucks and emergency response crews struggled to help the citizens in need because most of the roads and highways were in shambles. Emergency crews wouldn't be able to save Barbara. The flying starfish creature flew above her, eclipsing her in its shadow. Before the starfish splashed back into the ocean, Barbara's heart stopped dead in her chest.

# Golden Gate Terror

"*Whoa, whoa, whoa shit!* Sorry for the crazy driving, folks. Jesus, did you see that thing? Holy mother of God!"

Arnold Goodman steered his cab towards the shoulder of the Golden Gate Bridge. The suspension bridge was jolted by the impact of the raging waves below. The other cars also pulled over in unison to the side, right after the giant geyser of water spewed from the depths of the Pacific Ocean. Arnold had seen many things in San Francisco he would rather not have seen, but this, *this*, topped everything in his prior life experience.

Arnold's patrons, a young couple who couldn't be older than twenty, stared in horror through the window with their eyes bulging from their sockets.

*They won't help me one damn bit*, Arnold thought. *Wet behind the ears, dry inside the brains. Young kids have no common sense or ability to think critically. Generation dumbasses, that's what they are. The "do everything for me" generation. I guess it's up to me to deal with this mess, as always.*

"Leave it to me, folks," Arnold said with incredible determination, "I'm not taking any chances. Whatever that was, it's not coming near us."

The cabbie dug under his seat for his .45 revolver.

"Stay in the cab, folks, I turned off the meter and I'll be right back."

Arnold thought the young couple was going to piss themselves. *Leave it to me*, he kept thinking. *Leave it to Arnold fucking Goodman to deal with the world's problems. Like always. Like fucking always.*

The geyser of water stopped spewing. The moment that happened, something blasted high up in the sky. Arnold swore it was a government aircraft of some kind. It was thin, aerodynamic, and made of shiny black material. Definitely an aircraft, Arnold thought.

*Figures. This is some kind of government testing ground. I'll not be a part of any cover up. I'll shove this .45 up their bureaucratic assholes, and I'll never stop popping rounds until every last one of 'em are dead. I don't care how many times I have to wipe the shit off my gun. You can't keep me silent. I know what I'm seeing, damn it. Arnold fucking Goodman can't be silenced.*

Arnold realized in the next moment that he was dead wrong about his observations.

This was no government aircraft.

The black mass was almost as long as the Golden Gate Bridge itself. It hovered over the bridge waiting. Arnold could hear air hiss through the numerous holes in its body. The hermetic pressure caused the water in the San Francisco Bay to boil.

Arnold fired four shots at the black mass. He ducked back into his cab when the mass lowered itself closer to the bridge. The bullets got the floating mass's attention, and it was not happy.

Arnold flipped the meter back on and started driving down the bridge. "I know when it's time to get the hell out of here. My watch says go! Strap your seatbelts on, kiddos!"

The couple in the back was screaming. Arnold said everything in his customer experience canon to calm them down. Nothing would work. Arnold's heart was running a marathon in his chest. He was almost to the point of losing his cool, too.

*The thing looks just like a giant string ray.*

*No damn way.*

The suction sound of air, like a hundred airplanes engines about to take off at once, kept increasing in power. So deafening, Arnold had to stop the car and cover his ears. Every window in the car burst. Glass shattered on the hundreds of vehicles scattered about the bridge.

Arnold ducked down when the hood and trunk of the cab were wrenched upwards and flung aside by the massive surges of air. Cyclone forces spun vehicles on their wheels. Some vehicles were pitched over the side of the bridge, flung like toy cars. The bridge became a deadly high-speed destruction derby of chaos.

Right when Arnold shouted, "Hold on, folks!" the top of the car was peeled back like a tin can. Arnold was lifted up so hard that it snapped the seatbelt restraining him. The young couple hadn't worn their seatbelts and were spring-ejected upwards immediately. Arnold did four upside down, right side up spins. Massive numbers of people were hovering in the air after being forcibly removed from their vehicles.

Arnold craned his neck as he was suctioned towards the string ray's body. Black sleek skin covered its underbelly, as did thousands of mouths with lips the texture of black licorice. Arnold was sucked head first into one of the champing maws and devoured alive.

Blood rained down upon the Golden Gate Bridge.

# Laguna Beach

Carter Johnson knew the pleasures of people watching. Skin, sin, and dumbass college students paraded Laguna Beach liquored up and ready to party. Carter owned three of the seaside resorts on the white sandy beach coast. It was four in the afternoon, and the party was just getting warmed up. Wet T-shirt contests, navel shots, booming bass party music, and the promise of sex and self-discovery filled the owner with a sense of immortality. Carter was sixty years old, but the crazy kidder felt like he was in his twenties, vicariously living through the youth surrounding him.

He was about to deliver free Jell-o shots to a pack of babes at the edge of the beach when he saw something happen so fast, he wasn't sure it even happened. Once he saw the sight of red tinge the otherwise crystal clear blue water, Carter dropped his tray of shots and reeled in horror.

A hideous mouth with shark teeth swept across the water and took in every swimmer. Over a hundred people were swallowed up in the giant maw in seconds. The mouth was the length of a bus! Carter saw a beady black eye, then a dorsal fin, and a tail that propelled the mega-ton mass with impossible agility to the other side of the beach.

Out the shark's gills, plumes of spurting blood spewed for over twenty yards. Carter heard bones crunching and screams abruptly snuffed out.

This shark had the body of a commercial cruiser. Its length was covered in thick bony scales colored in green sea muck. It created a deep-sea camouflage color scheme over its body. The shark looked like an ancient sea monster.

The shark arched its body and made another b-line for the swimmer's it had missed. Carter sprinted into the main building to call for help when something sticky slapped his back. His feet left the ground. His limbs swatted helplessly at empty air. Carter could only see streaks of fast movement. Higher and higher, he was being hoisted. Carter couldn't move. The stuff on his back was like glue. He imagined himself a fly stuck on flypaper.

Carter looked down. He was being carried well above the height of a skyscraper. He was looking down at Orange County with a bird's eye perspective. Then he witnessed something that made him forget about the prehistoric looking shark in the water.

Eight tentacles were sweeping the streets. The side of the tentacles with the sticky nodules were slapping down on roads, sidewalks, and streets, and grabbing people up into the air. Fifty people were stuck to each tentacle, screaming and calling out for help. Carter saw bodies thrash above and below him.

The hideous squid was all black with a white underbelly. Those eyes glowed an unnatural ruby red color. Below the eyes, a giant mouth opened. The reek of salt water, rotten fish, and ice-cold air struck Carter. He didn't have a chance to experience the full effect, for the tentacle he was stuck on flexed, shifted, and swung. Carter was thrown into the squid's gaping mouth like a piece of popcorn. His body clashed mid-air with the dozen other victims on their way to being devoured. Carter's skull hit another man's skull, and it was lights out for the both of them.

# Trance

Junior Dempkey had a fetish, and Junior was quite proud of that fetish. The problem with every fetish was introducing the concept to the opposite sex and having them agree to the terms. Junior received many slaps to the face and punches to the stomach in his time. However, Holly Knox wasn't like every woman. She was game for anything, including Junior's special fetish: screwing women in open windows. Holly had her top half sticking out of his sixth story apartment building in San Diego. Junior was pumping her hard doggy style. There was nothing like the thrill of someone from another building spotting them. The thrill and adrenaline was a freakin' rush of testosterone boiling in his balls.

Holly stopped enjoying their sex. "Junior, we have to stop!"

"What, somebody spot us? What are they going to do? Pick us out of the many apartments in this building and have us arrested? They can't do anything. I'm not stopping for anybody. Once I'm in, *I'm in*."

Holly's body seemed to go stiff. Her head was craned up to the sky. Her face was in awe of what glowed neon pink from up in the sky.

"Holly, you okay? Hey, Holly? Hello, my dick is in you. Care to take notice?"

Junior shook her and waved his hand in front of her face. He felt like an idiot doing this from a doggy position. Holly's eyes were unblinking. She didn't respond to anything.

Junior turned his neck just right to see what was so spectacular. The neon pink colors were coming from a colossal-sized jellyfish floating in the air. The glowing pink ball spread its magnificent colors over the city. People on the streets and in their homes had stopped to appreciate the sight.

There wasn't fear in their eyes.

It was awe.

What nobody saw barreling into the city was the four-headed tortoise with the shell made of the thickest bone. The mega-ton turtle stomped into the city, causing every building to shift and nearly topple. The four turtleheads kept gnashing at the air with mouths that were bloodthirsty and hungry. The mouths dripped saliva down upon the city like a sick rain. Then the head and legs retracted into its body. The shell flew from one city block to another, spinning and smashing through buildings with the speed of a bullet. The wrecking turtle cleared the way for its counterpart to take action.

As the people of San Diego, including Junior and Holly, stared at the pink color, the jellyfish swooped down, sucked up the wreckage of entire buildings, and swallowed everything up. Out its back end, concrete, brick, and steel were shot out like excreted matter. The victims were kept inside its see-through body, where thousands kept beholding the power of the pink light. Soon, digestive juices turned those people into liquid protein.

The city of San Diego never stood a chance.

# The Reports Are In

*Kristie Gaines*
*News Channel Eight Report*

"This is Kristie Gaines for News Channel Eight. As you can see behind me, the entire city of San Francisco is in flames. Every person in direct vicinity of the Golden Gate Bridge has disappeared. Sightings of a flying object have been reported to the authorities. Valid sources claim a monster in the sky has torn the roofs off homes and attacked residents. So far, the local authorities and the military have failed to control the situation. Meanwhile, San Francisco is a disaster area."

*Text Message:*
*Tori, don't go outside. There's a giant fucking turtle in your backyard!*

*Frank Turner*
*CNN Correspondent*
*Special Report*

"All along the Pacific coastline, cities are under siege by sea monsters. This is not a hoax. According to scientists, prehistoric monsters have broken free of the ocean floor and are rampaging the city streets. We are their food. We are their prey. Everybody is in danger. We are at the very bottom of the food chain. Hey, don't push me out of my seat. I'm telling the citizens the truth. We are all in danger. You can't stop me from what I'm trying to tell the world. We shall be eaten if our military doesn't put a stop to this awful carnage! Save yourselves. WE ARE THEIR FOOD!"

*Gloria Tanner*

*Channel Four News Field Correspondent*

"Attack jets have cleared the affected west coast areas. It appears the missile attacks are slowing the monsters down. They've retreated into the ocean. The California coast has been declared a disaster area. Citizens have been relocated. The unbelievable events are coming to a close. The area is safe, but for how long?"

*Private Conversation between President Ted Yearling and Naval Defense Coordinator Captain Guy Mendel*

President Yearling: "We can't have unsubstantiated reports of monster attacks driving our country into a frenzy. First, I have to confirm the stories. Is this really happening?"

Captain Mendel: "The reports are verified. Aquatic enemies from the ocean are attacking the west coast. The causalities are mounting. Entire cities along the California Coast are simply...gone."

President Yearling: "I depend on you to advise me, Captain. Americans think I have my thumb up my ass. Tell me what to do and I'll sign the order. Any plan, I'll back you up. My only requirement, just make the killing stop."

Captain Mendel: "Yes, sir. Of course, sir. I know what to do. We've had a secret committee researching the ocean floor. There has been a looming threat down there for centuries. They've anticipated one day that this might happen. Our reservations on acting on this threat may have cost millions of people their lives. My advice, we strike back hard. Our naval forces and air forces are ready to be deployed, but there's one thing I need you to understand."

President Yearling: "What's that, Captain? Make it quick. We're wasting valuable time."

Captain Mendel: "We have to use the super sub. You remember The Annihilator?"

President Yearling: (sighing hard) "Of course, I do. I thought that project was scraped. It cost too much, and there wasn't a threat to use it against. It was a waste of tax dollars. Iraq was already costing us an arm and a leg."

Captain Mendel: "Well, there's a threat now. We've got The Annihilator on reserve. There's only one of its kind remaining. The rest of the subs were left incomplete. It's the only way to stop our real enemy. Gargantuan. That's what the scientists have named the creature that's broken free of the ocean floor approximately six hours ago. The monsters that attacked the city were Gargantuan's spawn. You stop Gargantuan, and you stop its spawn. The Annihilator is our only hope."

President Yearling: "But that's a nuclear sub. We can't unleash nukes on American soil."

Captain Mendel: "This will all take place under the ocean. I promise taking the risk is absolutely necessary."

President Yearling: "Then deploy, Captain. Do whatever's necessary. If we contaminate the ocean, we can fix it somehow, but if everybody's dead, what does a little pollution matter?"

Captain Mendel: "One more thing, sir."

President Yearling: "Yes, anything."

Captain Mendel: "We need Andrew Stevens."

President Yearling: "You mean, *the* Andrew Stevens?"

Captain Mendel: "Yes, I'm talking about Anchor Stevens. Anchor's the only one who can pilot the Annihilator. Okay, a few others can pilot it, but nobody can steer that sub like Anchor can."

President Yearling: "I never thought we'd be in this situation. Things are coming back to bite us in the ass. Just when you thought you buried someone under the system, they come back. What else can we do? Goddamn it. What choice do I have? The nation's about to jump out of their skins. These monsters have the nation by the balls. I can't hold off on the decision. I'll sign the order. Just do what you need to do, Captain. I put my trust fully in you. Remember, my term's up in a year. I'll promote you if all goes well. This could help or cripple my political future. If you need Anchor, you got him. Just end this as soon as possible. *I want every monster crushed.*"

State of Emergency Presidential Address

"Yesterday was a somber day, my fellow Americans. Our nation has lost millions of brave Americans in a vicious attack along the California Coast. This violence came swiftly and without warning. This unbelievable enemy owns no moral compass. Know this; our Navy is ready to squash this threat on all levels. Our Air Force has forced the enemy back into the water, and we're taking the battle to the Pacific Ocean. We will not relent. We must prevail. This aquatic menace must, and shall be, destroyed. Mark my words, Gargantuan doesn't stand a chance against our subs. Come hell or high water, our shores will be safe again. Nobody, and I mean nobody, dares to steal America's freedom. Human or monster be damned!"

# PART TWO: PREPARE FOR BATTLE

# Anchor Stevens

Anchor Stevens was lying prone on a cot. His head was as heavy as an anvil from a pounding migraine. This was a drug-induced pain. Anchor knew it, because this wasn't the first time this ex-naval officer had been drugged and taken somewhere against his will. This was an officer's quarters in a submarine. Steel walls painted dark blue surrounded him. He was used to the claustrophobic walls. Anchor had spent the last year in a private government prison compound. However, this wasn't his prison cell. Anchor's cell had a window with a view of the ocean and the sun. His freedom lay far beyond those waters, long forgotten. America had taken his freedom away from him and wouldn't give it back. He was another victim of Naval Defense Coordinator, Captain Guy Mendel's, bullshit bureaucracy.

So, what was he doing on a submarine instead of rotting in a secret prison?

This was about to get very interesting.

"Get up, Anchor. We have little time to work with. We're already on our way to the battle zone. There's much to cover if you're going to pilot The Annihilator."

Anchor recognized that voice. The sound of it made his guts tighten and his fists clench. He ignored the wave of migraine pain in his skull and sat on the edge of the cot. Against the wall was a TV monitor showing that ugly face.

Captain Mendel.

The conniving bastard.

Mendel was the embodiment of smug. The Naval Defense Coordinator, and special advisor to the President of the United States, was in his late sixties. He had a shaved head and was always sucking on the nub of an unlit cigar. *Just light the Goddamn thing*, Anchor thought, *or shove it up your tight ass.*

Mendel worked among the government's elite. Secret Service, CIA, FBI, any branch of National Security, Mendel has his hand in the action. He had enough power to bury people under the system, including Anchor. Anchor thought being framed for mass murder and having your life taken away from you was something out of fiction. To have it happen to him, it was to steal a man's soul, and Mendel was the type never to give a man's soul back, unless...

"What do you want from me, Mendel? You've already taken everything away from me that's worth taking. What else is there to squeeze from me?"

"There's no time for petty bickering, Anchor. Considering the circumstances, you could've been tried for treason and executed, and I'm not talking about a hood over the head and a bullet scenario. I'm talking about the *private* executions. The type where they shove sawdust into your eyes until you die of shock. Yeah, our country still does that in case you dare question me. I've sat ringside to many foreign terrorists executions with a bag of popcorn in my hands and a big ol' smile on my face."

"Cut the hot shot talk, Mendel." Every word out of Mendel's mouth was another reminder of what he'd lost and how powerless Anchor was to get it back. "I had nothing to do with what happened on the Atlantic Ocean. Pretty boy, Peter Olsen was drunk on that submarine I was piloting. He was the one who fired that missile at that cruise ship and killed almost five hundred innocent people. If Olsen wasn't the president's son at the time, I wouldn't be the one charged with the crime. I know the truth, and so do you, Captain. You haven't done me any favors."

Mendel made a disgusted face.

The captain didn't want to say what he was about to disclose.

"Unfortunately, our country has to make decisions that benefit the majority and harm the minority. It's how the world works. Right and wrong have no place in politics and national security. That said, you have a chance to clear your name. My hands are tied big time. Circumstances, for once, are working in your favor, Anchor. If you survive this assignment, you'll have a mountain of paper work to sign and disclosure forms to honor. Yes, you complete the mission, your name will be cleared, and you'll have your freedom back. Imagine being with your wife again."

The way Mendel smiled, Anchor knew none of this was true. Even if he could have his wife back, she had sent him divorce papers for him to sign a year ago. She said she didn't want to be married to a killer. Angela had remarried too. Angela had done something else to let Anchor know their marriage was over.

Anchor held back his tears thinking about what Angela did to hurt him. He struck it from his mind like all the other times the emotions became too much to handle. He would never get his life back the way it had been, no matter what happened. The opportunity was gone forever. Mendel could go fist fuck himself with those kinds of promises.

"You're a liar," Anchor accused, "I'm being used. Be honest with me. Leave the bullshit where it belongs, back in Washington. I have no use for it. Why am I on this submarine against my will?"

The monitor's screen changed from Mendel's face to various news reports and footage. The clips showed giant insane monsters ravaging the California Coast. Anchor forgot everything about his own personal hell and couldn't believe what he was viewing.

"Millions are dead, Anchor. It turns out we've got a big problem, and it's lurking in the ocean. Once we get closer to the source, I want you to pilot The Annihilator. I want you to destroy this threat. You're the best man for the job. The only one, in my opinion."

"I'm on the Annihilator?" Anchor couldn't handle each new piece of shocking information. He was breathing hard without realizing it. His chest went tight. "I thought the sub was junked after pretty boy Olsen blew that cruise ship to pieces."

"The project was terminated. Only one sub was completed, and that's the one you're on right now," Mendel explained. "I have a paranormal marine biologist/paleontologist on board to get you up to speed on the nature of the enemy, and how we're going to stop it. I need your full cooperation. You're the best pilot for this mission. You can steer this bad boy to victory."

"What the hell's a paranormal marine biologist?"

"You'll be finding out."

"What if I say no to your mission?"

"The United States, the entire world, could suffer many more casualties before we see the end of this, if not the complete destruction of every human being on this planet. This is the quickest way to snuff out the problem. May I remind you that your freedom is at stake? Imagine having your name cleared and being returned to your family. The rewards are there. You're a donkey, and I'm waving a carrot in your face. Take the carrot, Anchor."

"Fuck you. Don't talk about my family. My wife thinks I'm a murderer. She's moved on. I'm dead to everybody who once cared about me."

"They won't think that anymore," Mendel said, with an evil grin. "You'll be decorated with every award of valor."

Anchor knew better. Once someone was buried under the system, they would stay that way forever. The government wouldn't own up to their mistakes.

"I told you to leave the bullshit where it belongs, Captain. I complete your mission, or get wasted trying. That's the set-up. Then if I do survive, you'll park my ass right back in that private government prison. No one would be the wiser. Fuck off. Put some other asshole in the pilot's seat."

Captain Mendel sucked on his cigar. Anchor could see it in the man's beady eyes, his anger at being told "no", and his desperation to smooth things over and somehow get what he wanted.

"I understand you're upset. Let me put it this way. Forget your freedom. Think about your wife. Even if your relationship is over, you still care about her well-being. She re-married, yes, and she's pregnant with her first child. Angela lives in San Jose. That's not very far at all from the coast. They're in as much danger of being slaughtered by this threat as everybody else. You say no, The Annihilator is a useless attack sub. You say yes, in the very least, you know you saved your wife and family from imminent harm. That's all I can promise you. I say that should be enough."

"You heartless bastard," Anchor growled. "Quit pretending like you understand human emotions. I'm a pawn in your game, and as always, you control the game. Fine. You make a damn good point, even if everything else you've said has been hot smoke blown up my asshole. Let's get on with this. Tell me what to do and get the hell out of my way, fuck face. I'm tired of looking at your ugly mule butt mug."

Captain Mendel told him what to do next.

# Fight

Anchor Stevens was given the simple instructions to exit the private quarters and step into the hallway. Before doing that, he doused his head with water in the sink. Peering into the mirror, Anchor saw the defeat etched into his features. He was twenty-five years old and looked to be in his late thirties. A year living in prison isolation would turn any healthy, sane person, into a haggard mess. The prison was designed so he didn't get to talk to anybody. He read books, lifted weights, ate terrible food, and thought about his wife and how Angela believed him to be a savage murderer.

The worse thing, when Angela wrote him a letter saying she wanted a divorce, she mentioned one detail that sealed the deal. Their divorce was final forever. Angela said she had been pregnant with Anchor's child in the letter. She aborted it shortly after the trial verdict was rendered. Anchor wasn't going to be a father. She had denied him the ultimate gift of bringing human life into the world.

So much weighed on his mind while in isolation. Bitterness, helplessness, thoughts of wanting to be dead overwhelmed him, and it would've consumed his ability to focus on the present if it weren't for one idea. He wasn't in his cell anymore. He was off the miserable remote prison island. Even if he was deep down in the ocean depths, this is where he did his best work. This was freedom, in a small way.

Anchor sucked in a deep breath and steeled himself for what was coming his way next. Outside his door stood two naval officers. The man and woman were dressed in traditional Navy attire. The man was a burly guy named Topper. The woman, who had the aura of intensity and intelligence, and the biggest tits he'd ever seen in the Navy, was named Bright. Anchor remembered

Topper and Bright from the special naval training classes. They were the best cadets, just as Anchor had been, about two years ago, when they had trained to operate the mega submarine called The Annihilator.

Before they could talk beyond introductions, another officer made his way down the narrow hallway.

*No.*

*Not him.*

*That fucker.*

Anchor went from one mode of hatred for Mendel and accelerated into an all-new height of rage.

"You son-of-a-bitch, how dare you show your face to me, I'll kill you with my bare hands!"

Anchor tightened his fist, cocked back his arm, and released the blow that would drop pretty boy Peter Olsen to the floor. Blood oozed from both of Olsen's nostrils. Anchor could see the stars twinkle in Olsen's eyes. Topper and Bright held Anchor back, because he was about to stomp Olsen's chest cavity in. Maybe he'd be lucky enough to smash his heart. Anchor could always hope.

Topper was a large man, being a muscle bound two-hundred and forty pounds. He was a sensible, no messing around kind of guy. "You got him good, Anchor. Olsen deserved it. I would've knocked his damn block off. Now leave the cockroach to be a cockroach. We don't like him either. We know the truth about all those people who were killed on that cruise liner."

Anchor almost lost himself to tears. He wouldn't admit it to anybody how good it felt for someone to validate his innocence.

Olsen was helped up to his feet by two other officers. One was Wolfe, an officer good with fixing problems with gadgets and electronics on a submarine, and Kipper, a man who could sink anything in the ocean, including any bottle of booze or woman of his choice.

Olsen was using an oily rag to stop his nose. He waved the officers to back away. "Everything's fine now, right, Anchor? You've got it out of your system. If we're going to work together, this had to happen."

"You deserve so much more, you puny grub worm."

Anchor expected Olsen to deny every accusation. Instead, Olsen asked Anchor to follow him down the hallway. "I want a word with Anchor for a moment, in private. Please."

The officers stared at Olsen as if he was crazy.

"It's fine. Anchor won't do anything else to me. He'll hear me out, won't you?"

Anchor could've told him the truth and said he couldn't control himself when it came to matters of kicking the pretty boy's ass, but he didn't say anything. Anchor's life was on the line, and so were these other officers who were good, honorable, worthy people. The faster they understood the mission, the better. Anchor's personal problems meant little in the face of world domination.

Olsen showed him to a private room up ahead. When the door closed, Olsen had a mix of fear and shame on his face. The room was a janitor's closet full of mops, buckets, and various cleaning agents. On one wall was a poster of a scantily clad woman with DD tits with the American flag wrapped around her voluptuous body.

"Before you say anything," Olsen said, "you need to hear this. It was my fault I unleashed a missile on that cruise ship. I wanted to confess and accept the blame for what I did right when it happened. I was drunk, cocky, and plain stupid. My father, against my wishes, pulled strings in Washington, and arranged for you to go down for my crime. I had nothing to do with that decision.

"Now that my dad's not the president anymore, I was told I had to be on board The Annihilator, or be executed in private. Captain Mendel said I would die a horrible death. I don't care about any of that. I volunteered to be on this vessel. I owe my country that much. I never wanted you to go down for my crime. I'm so sorry, Anchor. It wasn't me who arranged for that to happen. My father abused his position as Executive-in-Chief. There was nothing I could do. I was both happy and upset to see you down here in the sub, Anchor. Happy, because I know you're one of the best people to pilot this sub. Sad, because—"

"You were afraid I would knock your head off."

Olsen shook his head.

"No.  Sad, because you deserve to live a happy and full life. It's going to be difficult to do that, considering this is basically a suicide mission."

# The Mission

Olsen was just like his politician father. The man knew how to craft words to make a point. The mention of this being a suicide mission downgraded Anchor from fighting mode to listening mode. Olsen showed him back into the main hallway where the rest of the officers were waiting. Olsen ushered them down the steel corridor among other lower ranking officers who were working in engineering, weapons, and general operations. The Annihilator was a different kind of attack submarine. Super submarine was an understatement. Anchor knew he'd be the one to oversee the piloting crew. Why else would the government work so hard to bring him here against his will?

First, Olsen explained, they were to have a short meeting with the paranormal marine biologist/paleontologist named Dr. Singer. This is where they were going now. Everybody filed into a larger conference room, be it narrow and cramped. There was a long table where everybody took a seat. The table had cookies, chips, and sodas. Dr. Singer, a tall and skinny man in his fifties, had a nervous excitement about him. The glasses he wore magnified his eyes to twice their size. It gave him a geeky, disturbing expression. He could've been a Nazi officer for The Third Reich, or a poorly adjusted computer programmer.

"Welcome everybody," Dr. Singer said, invitingly, "we have much to cover. Enjoy some snacks. It's not much, but I hope it helps you pay attention. Studies show it does. I'd put chips and soda in every classroom if it were up to me."

Topper was the first to sit down, pop open a soda, and eat from a bowl of chips. Bright poured others some coffee, and when it came Anchor's turn for a cup, she seemed nervous at his approach. Anchor picked up on that from people. They thought he was a killer, even when information contradicted the fact. A piece of information that had been in their heads for so long, Anchor understood, people had a hard time letting go of it. The cruise liner deaths were a huge media story. The story was plastered on every news forum for weeks.

Anchor skipped any polite pretense. "You think I killed those people on that cruise ship, don't you? I didn't. Talk to Olsen. He'll give you the details. Thanks for the coffee. I always take mine with way too much sugar."

Anchor sat down at the head of the table closest to Dr. Singer. Bright sat behind Anchor. He sensed her eyes on him. An apology was in her eyes, but she was too afraid to speak to him. Anchor knew he looked like shit. His ragged beard and desperate eyes made him look like a hobo with a heroin habit.

"Okay, everybody comfortable?" Dr. Singer asked everybody. "I'll make this quick. We have a lot to cover. Thank you for your bravery, and for volunteering for this highly dangerous mission. I know some of you weren't exactly volunteers."

Anchor wondered who else was forced onto this submarine against their will.

"The picking pool was small in selecting the pilots to helm The Annihilator. As you know, you, the select few, were specially trained to pilot this sub on attack mode. The Annihilator has many unique killing abilities. You were trained how to operate this machine, but you weren't informed on what kind of enemy you'd be going up against. There was good reason not to reveal sensitive classified information until the time was right. Olsen, could you dim the lights?"

Olsen dimmed the lights.

Dr. Singer began the power point presentation. Everybody stared at the image projected on the wall. The first image was a computerized sketch of the ocean floor.

"Over the past two decades, scientists have been eying the odd shifting of plate tectonics along the Pacific Ocean. There's been strange activity beneath the ocean floor. We've developed a special camera to take pictures and investigate what's beneath the ocean floor itself, and what we found was quite...alarming."

Dr. Singer changed images.

The next part of the presentation showed a large mass, the color of dark purple muscle tissue. The picture was very dark, and the details were blurry.

"This is the best shot we've been able to get of her."

"Her, who?" Anchor asked.

"Gargantuan."

Anchor would've dismissed the idea of monster attacks as a scientific fabrication, but he remembered the news footage Captain Mendel showed him of the California Coast and the monsters in action. Everybody else was of the same mind.

Sea monsters do exist.

Move on.

Dr. Singer continued his presentation.

"Gargantuan is a mega mass of tissue, muscle, bone, and reproductive organs. She dates back to Paleozoic Era. Think Cambrian Period. During this period, there was an explosion of life forms. At that time in history, deep in the ocean, Gargantuan was birthing deep-sea predators of many varieties. Every creature that's birthed from her body is pure evil. The spawn consume, terrorize, and seek to depopulate any local life to gain dominion.

"All we know, is that Gargantuan was somehow buried beneath the ocean floor at some point. She's been hibernating all this time, waiting for her chance to return. The last earthquake in California seemed to open up the ocean floor just enough for her to escape.

"The thing is, Gargantuan likes to study existing life forms and create hyper forms of those species. Yesterday, we witnessed a blown up version of a stingray, a jellyfish, a squid, and turtle, and so on. Gargantuan's main goal is to create life, consume, and destroy.

"Her offspring collect flesh, blood, and meat, and bring it back to her. Gargantuan turns this matter into digestible proteins for itself, and for her children. If we destroy Gargantuan, her offspring starve. Currently, she's situated deep in the Pacific Ocean. We've pinpointed her exact location. We're headed there as we speak. So that's the quick history of our enemy."

Kipper, even cockier than pretty boy Olsen, spoke up. "So, okay, that's all good and interesting, but how do we destroy this bitch? I really don't need to hear her life story. All I have to do is point and shoot, right?"

Dr. Singer smiled. "I was just about to get to that matter."

# So How Do We Destroy This Bitch?

Anchor refilled his coffee, opened up four packets of sugar, and sucked down a hot concoction of sweet caffeine, as Dr. Singer changed gears in his power point presentation.

"How do we stop this bitch? Indeed. It's a tall order, but one that's not impossible. I've been coached on the game plan, and it's a good plan. That's if it's executed properly. No mistakes. This isn't a field test."

"Come on, buddy," Wolfe said, "I volunteered for this mission. My entire family was killed in San Francisco. Let me at her. I'll take Gargantuan down a peg. I'll shove a nuke up that bitch's ass."

"Yeah, I lost my family too," Topper said. "I was laying out on the beach one moment, the next, my fiancée's in the mouth of that mega huge shark. She didn't stand a chance, and neither will Gargantuan when I'm done with her."

"The Annihilator will do its job if we're the ones in the driver's seat," Kipper boasted. "Lock on target and fire. All that will be left of her will be fodder for a cheap seafood buffet."

Only Anchor heard Bright whisper to herself. "*You're forgetting how many millions of people have been killed. This isn't a joke. This isn't a revenge party. It's a job. There's nothing fun about this mission.*"

Anchor looked about the room. These officers were scared out of their minds. He could see right through their false bravado. If he was going to risk his life, he had to level them out. Anchor agreed with Bright's quiet assessment.

"I'm sure if all it took was jamming a nuke up Gargantuan's asshole, we would've done it already," Anchor said, making everybody go silent with his commanding voice. "There's a catch. Let Dr. Singer give his presentation. Get your heads out of your asses. I'm not dying because of somebody else's fuck up. I've already sacrificed my life for Olsen's fuck up. It'll never happen again. Try me, and you'll be sorry."

Olsen gave Anchor a hard look, but the pretty boy didn't say anything.

Dr. Singer cleared his throat.

"Anchor is right. We can't shoot a nuke at her. Where Gargantuan dwells in the ocean, she's got a force field surrounding her. It'll turn any explosion, any source of heat or energy, into fuel. If anything touches that force field, an electrical surge will turn a submarine and its cadets inside into a deep fat fryer. The attack can't be from the outside. It has to be from within."

"Whoa, wait up, Dr. Singer," Topper said, crunching on a mouthful of chips. "We're going *inside* of Gargantuan?"

"What about that force field?" Olsen asked, trying to subdue everybody's overreaction. "There's a way to get past it, right?"

Dr. Singer rubbed at his tired eyes. Anchor could tell the scientist had been up for days trying to help map out an attack plan. Beneath the fatigue, Anchor could tell Singer was still hungry for the destruction of Gargantuan.

"Hear him out, no more interruptions or shitting your pants," Anchor said. "We're the best of the best, got that? Quit acting like a bunch of spoiled children. I'm not wiping anybody's ass, and nobody's wiping mine. We have the capability of killing this thing, and we will. Stay focused. Go ahead, Dr. Singer."

"Thank you, Anchor. As I was saying, the real battle will be within Gargantuan. She's a complex mega organism. Imagine her as a giant hive full of complicated organs, processes, and abilities. She can give birth to anything her mind conceives. She's a reproductive machine. It takes other organisms to work that machine, and Gargantuan is full of them.

"So, Gargantuan is filled with other creatures that are working behind the scenes to make everything possible. The Annihilator will have to get inside as close to Gargantuan's core as possible. Once inside, we set up several explosive charges scattered about her networks of tissue, then we escape using The Annihilator. We'll set off those nuclear charges by remote."

Kipper was frustrated. "This is a suicide mission. This is bullshit. Go inside Gargantuan? I mean, damn. We're not getting out if we're going in."

Dr. Singer disagreed. "It's not bullshit. I'm going in with you. Did you care to think I've thought through every possible contingency to allow us to survive? You bet. Your life will be in your own hands. The risk is high, but we're all dead anyway if Gargantuan isn't stopped. We might not even make it through that force field. We could die on the way to Gargantuan's core. We could be attacked by God knows what while placing those charges once we leave the sub. A myriad of possibilities of death could occur, and I don't care, because we have to give this our best shot. I'm willing to die if it means saving the world, and I'm just a scientist. If I'm not afraid, why are you?"

Anchor sensed the tension in the room. People who served their country could claim they would do anything for that piece of land, but they were still people, and people feared death. It's what else a soldier had inside them to cope with death that made them who they were. This was a question of guts and balls. Who had them, and who didn't?

The only person Anchor sensed wasn't afraid to die, besides Dr. Singer, was Bright. She was a student taking notes, paying attention, and eager to get to work. Even Topper had stopped mowing down on the snacks once the truth set in. They would most likely die carrying out this mission.

Dr. Singer had one other thing to say.

"Remember the force field I mentioned? We've learned whenever missiles are shot at it, small holes in the force field form. We'll have to find a hole in that force field, move past it, and then enter Gargantuan. A fleet of submarines will back us up. Call them a distraction to help us complete our mission by any means necessary, people. I'm sorry I can't be more hopeful. I'm willing to put my life on the line for the cause. I sure hope you are too."

Another long silence filled the room.

Dr. Singer dismissed everybody, except for Anchor.

"Can I have a word, Anchor. I just have a few things to go over with you."

# Leadership

Dr. Singer didn't waste a second sharing what was on his mind. "A lot's on the line, Anchor, and I'm glad you're here. I've been trained on the details of The Annihilator's killing abilities. It's quite the submarine. It's like nothing I've ever encountered before. Another one's being made as we speak, but it takes a lot of time. It'll be too late before a second is functional to help us now. A machine of that caliber can't exactly be thrown together like a sandwich."

Anchor wasn't sure where the scientist was going with this talk. Dr. Singer sensed his patience dwindling and jumped to the point.

"You're going to be the first in command. It's up to you to make sure we get past that force field, sneak inside Gargantuan, and set those explosions. You understand our survival comes second to completing this mission, don't you?"

"Of course."

"Very good. I knew you would understand. I'll be your wingman. I've been schooled on every weapon and ability The Annihilator possesses. I can pilot the vessel as well. You keep your crew focused, I'll keep you in the know. I think we're of one mind on this. I will do anything and everything possible to complete the mission and keep everybody alive. I need your full cooperation. Deal?"

Anchor shook the scientist's hand. "Deal."

"The Annihilator's being controlled by a temporary crew. We've got a short period of time before we have to take our stations. I want you to talk to our crew and make sure they've got their heads screwed on right. I saw the looks on their faces. They weren't exactly thrilled."

"I got it," Anchor said, "no worries."

"I've seen a lot over the years. Alien life forms from below the ocean and from up in the skies. If we fail, Gargantuan could possibly kill every person in the entire universe. Much is at stake. Everything, actually."

Anchor didn't care about the big picture.

Now mattered.

Tomorrow, he would deal with later.

"Things are going to get hairy once we get inside the beast and take it on foot. We've got weapons and suits none of you are used to wearing. This mission has been thrown together in a great hurry. The real problem, our government never thought Gargantuan would break through the ocean floor. No matter what I told them, they were only willing to throw a limited amount of funds to counter the problem. Looks like innocent people have to pay the price."

"It's always up to people like us to fix other people's mistakes. I'm as good as dead, Dr. Singer. I have nothing to fear. I can learn in a hurry. So can the rest of the crew."

"Good to hear. Oh, and one other thing," Dr. Singer said, "you keep smiling. Are you enjoying this?"

"I've been locked up in isolation for over a year, Dr. Singer. So right now, I feel like I'm on a fucking playground. So yeah, this is all shits and giggles."

# Sexual Harassment

"Come on, Bright? One last goodbye to the world fuck. How about it? The world's on the brink of destruction. Imagine the adrenaline rush. My cock. Your pussy. Boom."

Anchor walked in on the crew standing crowded together outside the conference room door. Kipper was in Bright's face, trying to sweet talk her in that special douche bag way. Anchor thought about intervening, and so did the other crew, but Anchor recognized something in Bright's face. She was strategizing and not backing down. Anchor motioned for the crew to back off, because he knew Bright wanted to take care of the creep herself.

"You're so quiet and serious all the time," Kipper continued. "You act like you have something lodged up your ass. Or do you need something up your ass? Maybe that's your problem. Either way, I've got what you need. You haven't changed since special training. Stiff as a pole. Let me loosen you up. You got those torpedo tits. We could fire those at Gargantuan and take her out right now."

Bright was giving him the steely eyes of death.

Kipper kept pulling items from his dirt bag of tricks.

"Hey, I'm not a jerk. I'm only trying to go out with a bang. Don't you want to go out with a bang?"

Bright shook her head. "Only a real son-of-a-bitch would use this situation to take advantage of a lady. Back off, dick face. I'm not interested. Get that through your thick skull before I crush it."

"Whoa, wait! You haven't given me a chance to win you over."

Kipper grabbed her arm to bring her in close.

Bright jerked her arm back, slipping free of his hold. Her hands were fists and her body was posed to counter anything. If Kipper came in close proximity, there would be a fight.

"Fuck off. The answer's no."

"Listen, there hasn't been a pussy I couldn't conquer," Kipper insisted. "Black pussy. White pussy. Yellow pussy. Hot sushi oriental pussy. Pussy of all flavors, colors, and sizes, I've fucking rocked them all. I don't care if I sound like a pervert. I love fucking. I want one last ride, and you've got the body of every man's dreams. Give me a shot. This is it. We're all probably dead. So why not fuck me? I'm not going to get you pregnant, and STD's, no sweat. We're goners. I'm the only guy with the balls to put it out there. Let's fuck. I know you want me too, so why not go for it?"

"Go jerk off in a waste basket, or better yet," Bright smiled, "stick your twig in a pencil sharpener until the tip is as pointy as your head."

Kipper wasn't a man who was used to being told no. He came from a rich family. Kipper had good looks, privilege, and he could sling the English to drop even the most reserved panties and score. Kipper had pulled the same excessive flirtations during their original training courses for The Annihilator two years ago. Kipper didn't compute rejection.

"Come on, baby. Playing hard to get is only fun for so long. It's time to give in."

Bright's face was hard. Anchor could see it in her eyes that she was secretly happy. Push me, those eyes said, and I get a warrant to kick your ass. "Still not getting the message, huh?"

"Persistence pays off, honey," Kipper insisted. "I'm not taking no for an answer. I'll fight off the rest of these bozos to win your honor. Come on. Let me have a taste of that sweet action. I'll bend you over like—"

Bright delivered a solid throat punch, then a fist to his solar plexus. Kipper's sexual come-ons degraded to the coughing up of blood. Bright thought that would've been enough. Anchor didn't even see it coming.

"You cock-teasing bitch, you can't do this to me!"

Kipper cold cocked her in the face. Bright lost her bearings and she was thrown backwards. She wasn't getting up from the floor anytime soon. Wolfe and Topper were tending to her.

*That's good*, Anchor thought, *because this guy's getting the whole can of whoop-ass.*

Kipper was standing there frozen. One reason, he couldn't believe he had decked Bright. Then Kipper met eyes with Anchor. He knew the beast was coming, and Kipper's lower lip trembled. The officer started to cower back in fear.

Anchor's voice was a hungry wolf's. "Where you going to hide? Going to jump out a window? We're in a submarine deep down in the ocean. There's nowhere for you to hide. Best take me on where you stand. You run, you're only going to piss me off even more, you wretched boar. I'll bash your face until your brains are pulp. Your dick will never work again, and the world will be a better place for it."

Kipper's face was locked in horror. "Look, I didn't mean to, Jesus, Anchor, don't do what I think you're about to do. I'll leave her alone. Hey, I'm sorry Bright. I had no right. I don't know what came over me, I—"

Anchor was taken aback by what happened.

Everybody else, including Bright, gasped in shock.

Nobody saw it coming.

Dr. Singer had crept up behind Kipper. The doctor's long and lanky arms worked with deadly precision. One hand snuck under Kipper's neck, and the other had him by the head. Then, SNAP! Lights out for Kipper. He collapsed as dead weight.

Anchor's body went from red hot with fury to icy cold with dread. Dr. Singer was a lunatic. The doctor regarded his act as necessary, almost clinical. This mission took on an entire new angle, and Anchor didn't like the smell of it.

"It's my fault for not emphasizing the importance of our work," Dr. Singer said calmly. "We are to conduct ourselves with valor. None of this indiscretion will be tolerated. I will replace Kipper and take on his duties. I can do his job just fine. It's a shame. That's more work on my plate. Oh well. It is what it is."

Topper, Olsen, and Wolfe, helped Bright up to her feet. They shielded her from Dr. Singer's path and from having full view of Kipper's corpse. Dr. Singer ordered a passing cadet to arrange for Kipper's body to be relocated.

Everybody stood rigid in place, including Anchor. Everybody was afraid to do the wrong thing, or else suffer the harsh consequences. Dr. Singer went from nerdy scholar to a calculating killer in seconds. There was a lot to the doctor that Anchor had yet to understand.

"I take it everybody understands they are to do their job, get along, and stay focused? The mission is all there is now. No goodbye last fucks, no time for anything else but doing your jobs."

Everybody said they understood.

"Very good. We shouldn't have anymore problems among each other now that the problem child has been punished." Dr. Singer checked his watch. "Looks like we better take to our battle stations. Follow me."

# Battle Stations

The rest of the eighty person crew were hard at work in different sectioned off chambers of the submarine keeping things functioning. The team avoided the crew, walked a short flight of stairs on the double decker submarine, and arrived at the front-most section of the submarine. During training, the cadets joked that the bridge looked like something out of *Star Trek*. The Annihilator was straight out of science fiction. There was a chair hanging in the center of the bridge, where the main pilot sat in front of a large screen that gave a panoramic view of the ocean ahead of them. Co-pilots obeyed the main pilot's instructions. Their stations were at the right and left of the main pilot. They operated weapons, monitored possible attacks, and ensured the vessel could withstand the intensity of battle. Glowing computer screens and blinking buttons busied the bridge. Everybody stood behind the doctor. The dark red room was intimidating to the crew who waited in anticipation for Dr. Singer to say what was on his mind.

"Anchor, you're the best cadet of your class. You take the main pilot's seat. I'll join Topper, Wolfe, Bright, and Olsen as your co-pilots. You direct traffic, Anchor. Our lives are in your hands. Everybody ready?"

Anchor didn't like the way Dr. Singer was taking charge. He also didn't like how the doctor made everybody nervous. The adrenaline was already running in their veins, pumping fear and jitters into their stressed out minds. The threat of murder by something other than Gargantuan and her spawn was the last thing they needed.

He had to set the crew at ease.

This required drastic action.

Anchor knew nothing of Dr. Singer's piloting abilities. There was risk in what Anchor was about to do, but it was an acceptable risk. Olsen, Wolfe, Topper, and Bright's faces were petrified.

"Dr. Singer. I'm going to ask you to stand down from the bridge. You can communicate to us from the other room. You can monitor everything we do from the equipment located in the backmost part of the bridge. The equipment's sufficient."

Dr. Singer's lips were drawn tight.

"Excuse me?"

"After breaking Kipper's neck, we're a little uneasy in your presence. I'm being direct because I don't want my pilots having nervous trigger fingers. I can do this without your assistance, Dr. Singer. You communicate with me directly, and only me. If you don't like it, you can try to break my neck, too. But I promise you, I won't go out like Kipper. I'll see you coming, and I guarantee you, you'll be the one who ends up dead. You want to help the mission, then you do as I suggest. Or are we going to waste time arguing?"

The screen showing the dark waters of the ocean suddenly switched to a different channel. There was Captain Mendel sitting in his office. He was alarmed by the scene taking place on the bridge.

"No, Anchor, you won't fight Dr. Singer. He's here to help. Dr. Singer needs to be right there with you on the bridge to ensure entry into Gargantuan is successful."

"Your scientist just snapped a man's neck," Anchor argued. "Yeah, Kipper was a jerk wad, but I'd say the punishment was a bit drastic, especially considering the circumstances. I don't trust the guy. I think I speak for everybody on that issue."

"It's not your job to question me, or Dr. Singer. Dr. Singer has worked very closely with us to ensure the mission is completed. You're in charge of your crew, Anchor, but Dr. Singer is in charge of you."

"I'm not taking orders from this murderer."

"Oh, yes you are." Captain Mendel's conniving smile spread across his louse face. He raised his hand. There was a black box with a blinking red dot. "I can end this mission right now if you and your crew don't plan on following orders. This black box can make The Annihilator go BOOM."

Anchor wanted to call the captain's bluff. That could prove dangerous, though. Captain Mendel had everything stacked in his favor.

Anchor could only say one thing.

"How can you reassure me and my crew that Dr. Singer won't try killing anyone else? If Gargantuan and her spawn are as deadly as they appear, this submarine is going to turn into a pressure cooker of nerves. I don't want my crew worrying about being killed while they pilot this thing."

Dr. Singer stepped in front of the screen. "I'll stay in the back of the bridge. I won't be in reach of your crew, Anchor. Look, we're wasting time here. I acted swiftly earlier in dealing with Kipper's unacceptable behavior. I'll keep my distance if it means getting on with the mission."

"Very good," Captain Mendel said, clutching the detonator with both hands. "If anything happens where I think this mission is compromised, I'll send you right in the direction of Gargantuan and turn this vessel into a kamikaze weapon. This is the best plan to fight Gargantuan for the moment. *For the moment.* There's always a Plan B. If our think tank comes up with a better idea, consider yourselves terminated."

Anchor heard the others gasp. Wolfe, Topper, Bright, and Olsen's eyes were glued to the screen. They couldn't see through the bullshit, Anchor thought. What a vote of confidence Captain Mendel was. The problem Anchor had with the threat, Captain Mendel did not intend to carry it out. The detonator was a toy. It probably operated his grandmother's dildo. He also noticed how Dr. Singer didn't stiffen up or change demeanor at the threat of being terminated. Dr. Singer and Captain Mendel were up to something. This was more than a seek and destroy mission, and Anchor would find out just what the hell was really going on here. In the meantime, he had to play along with the plan.

"He can stay on the bridge," Anchor said to Mendel. "He can be right in the thick of it with us. The catch, if someone does something punishable, I'm the one to dole that punishment out. Dr. Singer is not to lay a finger on any of my crew. Is that fair?"

"Fair enough," Captain Mendel said. Whether the guy meant it or not was another matter. "On with the mission. You're in close proximity to Gargantuan. Good luck completing the mission. The whole world is counting on you."

The screen switched back to the view of the ocean. The dark depth of the sea was suddenly bright with strange lights and moving shapes.

They were closing in on Gargantuan.

The shit was about to hit the fan.

# Take Her In

"Take you battle positions," Anchor ordered, "everybody claim your assignment."

Topper, "Rear weapons."

Bright, "Front weapons."

Wolfe, "Right flank weapons."

Olsen, "Left flank weapons."

Dr. Singer, "Prime directive."

The crew was sitting in front of their control stations with their headsets on. Anchor was the maestro to this battle, sitting from the seat suspended from the ceiling in front of a control panel. He had to tell everybody what to do and when to do it. Anchor pressed his fingers on the panel so he could get a closer view of what was up ahead of them on the screen.

The Aqua Scope camera closed in too tight. Anchor was taken aback by the sight. A giant manta ray was floating in front of a wall of purple muscle tissue covered in black algae. That tissue wall was a section of Gargantuan. She was a meatball of gills, scales, bone, stringy flagellum, tracks of coral reef, and bubbles of fat, gnarly teeth with no mouth or apparent function, and reptilian plates. Craters, dips, and hollows without obvious function appeared; as if they were mouths disguised as innocent shadows. God took every deep-sea creature and waded them up into one nasty ball.

Anchor focused on the giant manta ray guarding Gargantuan. A slit opened in the algae wall of its underbelly, showing a pink recess. Once that recess opened wide like a mouth, holes in the manta ray's body forced out flaccid dead human corpses by the hundreds. The limp bodies were sucked inside Gargantuan by an invisible vacuum of air. The vacuum sounded like a note of rumbling thunder carried on for minutes at a time. Bodies kept leaving the manta ray's body and entering Gargantuan.

"Pan back Aqua Scope," Anchor said to Bright. "Let's get a wider view of this monster."

Bright did her job. The image on the large screen showed Gargantuan in her entirety. She was an even bigger ball of gnarly tissue covered in algae, jagged fish scales, and bone. The sheer size of Gargantuan was alarming.

Dr. Singer whistled. "She's as big as advertised. Gargantuan would take up twelve city blocks, and she'd be taller than three Sears towers combined. Gargantuan is tons and tons of power. Don't take her lightly."

"We weren't planning on it," Anchor said. "What are those tubes sticking out of her?"

There were long orange colored tubes. They resembled giant intestines that stretched for half a mile. From within the vascular tubes, bright lights were glowing. Those tubes were connected to other floating creatures that floated in circular fashion around Gargantuan.

"Those tubes feed energy to Gargantuan's spawn," Dr. Singer explained. "Let me adjust Aqua Scope so you can see it up close."

The tubes were shown in high clarity. The orange was amphibious skin. A gelatinous muck covered the tubes. Anchor imagined KY Jelly. Strange arteries and veins seemed to light up with sparks and jolts of visible blue electricity. Blue currents surrounded Gargantuan's body in moving forks and branches of high voltage.

"That manta ray is feeding Gargantuan human bodies. Gargantuan processes the flesh and blood and turns them into food for her children. The moment anything approaches too close, Gargantuan will cut her children loose to protect herself from any harm. That electric force field you see now will surround her until the battle is done. She's a real work of biology."

"I bet she has a nice pair of legs beneath all of that hideous flesh and sinew," Anchor said. "Enough admiring this fish bitch. Let's grind her up into cat food."

Communication was coming in from Captain Mendel.

"A fleet of attack submarines are fast approaching. Hold your position until the force field can be breached. Our subs are tracking the energy fields around Gargantuan. We'll give you the coordinates on the best course of entry once the intelligence is in."

"Hold positions," Anchor told his crew. "Sit tight."

A fleet of attack submarines was an understatement. Every submarine the navy owned, it seemed, was coming in for battle. Hundreds and hundreds of speeding streaks of steel were ready to subdue the beast. Foreign vessels met up with American submarines to take on a threat everybody could agree needed to be destroyed.

Anchor could only view the battle on the screen.

The problem, this wouldn't be a battle.

This would be a slaughter.

# Submarine Slaughter

Gargantuan came alive in the face of the submarine fleet. Anchor and the rest of the crew were blinded by the surge of retina-scorching electricity flowing and crackling around the monstrous ball. Currents of blue forks flowed around the beast like moving death threads. The threads kept flowing continuously at infinite speeds. The dark depths of the ocean were banished by the bright movements of energy. Anchor and his crew could only watch what played out on the battlefield from the sidelines. Each orange tube connected to Gargantuan's spawn retracted back into the body. The released spawn threaded through the lightning branches of electricity to take on the challenging fleet of submarines head on.

A squid the size of five hundred submarines put together, swatted its tentacle arms and exploded an entire wall of attack subs. Each vessel exploded with a muted BOOM followed by a short-lived ball of flames. A jellyfish creature appeared, shedding brilliant pink neon light onto the scene. Out from its clear body shot a net of pulsating pink color. That net wrapped around fifty submarines, collected them, and tucked the net back into its body. Anchor could see through the jellyfish's see-through mass, as submarines crashed against each other, blanketing one another in flames as steel crumbled under extreme cabin pressure.

"Holy fuck!" Olsen cried out. "Did you see that? Those subs were nothing against those creatures. We're like bathtub toys."

"We don't stand a chance," Topper rasped. He couldn't restrain the horror in his voice. "We're as good as dead. *Gawd-damn*."

Wolfe was frozen at his station. "The Annihilator's a joke. We're the ones that's going to be annihilated. We're fish food. We're fucking done."

"Shut up," Anchor barked, "can't you see those subs are just a distraction? They're being used. We're not the kamikazes. They are. That's the real problem here. Nobody's life should be carelessly thrown away for any cause. There's always a better way."

"Everybody here is being treated like kamikazes," Bright said. She wasn't fearful. The tough broad was just like Anchor: pissed off and hating those in charge. "I'm not letting this happen. We have to help them. The Annihilator is equipped with higher power weaponry. We can take these things on, damn it. We're not a bathtub toy. This machine can sink any machine or monster."

Dr. Singer intervened. "Yes, that's correct, it can, but we stay with the plan. Once an opening appears in the force field, we forge right through it. We don't engage in battle. If this submarine is taken down, all of our work has been for nothing."

"And let more people die?" Bright questioned. "No, I refuse. Who's with me? I'm not sitting here and taking this shit."

Anchor knew Bright was correct.

They couldn't watch their fellow officers die in battle.

"Prepare to engage weapons," Anchor said. "Let's show these monsters what we can do. *It's time to drop the anchor on these bastards.*"

Dr. Singer called Dr. Mendel on his headset. "They're not going with the plan, Captain. I can't reason with them. I mean, what else can I do to make them understand? We're on the brink of extinction, and—"

Anchor bolted up from his chair. Rushing to the other side of the bridge, he lifted Dr. Singer from his chair and head butted him. The scientist went unconscious instantly. He lay sprawled on the ground unmoving.

"Take a nap, ass wipe."

Captain Mendel appeared on the screen. "Anchor, you can't do this! We need Dr. Singer to advise you. This is not negotiable."

Anchor flipped Captain Mendel the finger. "Advise this. Sit on it and spin. I'll get inside that bitch, set off those charges, and save the day, but you can't expect me to watch this battle unfold without helping. Now get off my screen so I can get to work. I'm tired of looking at your sorry ass."

"I'll blow this ship up." Captain Mendel showed the detonator box in his hands. "Back down, or else. I mean it. You're not our only plan. You're just the best one for the moment. Go ahead and try me. I'll blow your submarine to pieces."

"The only thing you're going to blow is yourself," Anchor growled. "I don't have time for empty threats. Now get off my screen, you puke-faced pug-ugly motherfucker! This is my sub, and I'll do with it as I see fit. My mission, my results. Didn't you hear me a second ago? Go blow yourself."

"Canceling Captain Mendel from our network," Wolfe said, typing away at the computer keys. "He'll unscramble my blocker eventually. It still buys us some time."

"Good work. I'll take what I can get," Anchor said. "Now we're a team. Let's save some lives, people. This fish bitch won't know what hit her."

Anchor returned to his station, hit the red button on his console, and out from the steel panel, a steering wheel popped up. Anchor gripped the steering wheel and prepared himself for speed and destruction.

The Annihilator entered the theatre of battle. Anchor swung the sub right, avoiding another sub that had broken in half and was hurtling in their direction fast. Soon, Anchor dodged yet another concern. A three-headed tortoise towered over them. The turtleheads kept going in and out of their shells like violent whack-a-moles. They were chomping down on each sub in their path. Mini explosions turned their green heads into two-second glowing light bulbs.

Anchor steered over and down, dodging one mouth, then went up and right to avoid the other two maws that threatened to champ down through steel. A wall of air pockets sent The Annihilator belly up. Anchor worked quick to right the sub. The submarine was barely a quarter the size of one of the tortoises' heads. He had to do something quick or end up dead.

"Bright, fire a series of time delayed missiles at them. Use the Sinkers!"

"Yes, sir! Sinkers coming right up."

Bright unleashed three Sinker missiles in the direction of the three-headed beast.

DA-DOOM! DA-DOOM! DA-DOOM!

Each turtle extended their wrinkly necks to swallow the missile. The monsters gulped them down like vitamins.

"That was a billion dollars a piece you just swallowed," Anchor cheered, "and it's worth every penny. Imagine an atom bomb dissolving in your head, fuckers! It's time to put you in a box and bury your sorry asses."

Seconds later, the Stingers did their job. The tortoises' heads went POP POP POP. Anchor imagined a cork shooting from a bottle of champagne. Instead of sparking champagne, plumes of gore colored the waters. Their shells went up into thousands of pieces. Anchor could hear the shell shrapnel scrape the outside of the submarine.

"Dodging down," Anchor said, pivoting the wheel. "The last thing we need is a hole in our sweet machine."

An enormous manta ray was swooping after them in hot pursuit. Mouths beneath its belly were sucking up the submarines in its way and spitting them right back out in fiery steel flotsam.

"Whoa, yeah, I think you pissed it off, Bright," Topper cheered. "I guess they didn't realize who they were fucking with, did they? America's going to stick its gun up your asses and pull the trigger."

Olsen remained focused. "Manta ray's in my sights."

"Don't waste anymore ammunition," Anchor instructed. "Wolfe, engage the blade. We're in science class, kids. It's dissection time. Only good, clean cuts. You open this fucker up, I'll give you an "A" for ass-kicking."

"Ready, Anchor!" Wolfe liked the choice of weapon, and it showed on his face. "Blade is engaged. Slice and dice. Your ass is sushi!"

Along The Annihilator's aerodynamic body, a long and thick blade appeared underneath the sub, giving the appearance of the bottom of an ice skate.

"Dropping down," Anchor said, engaging the submarine to lower five hundred feet in mere seconds. He tipped The

Annihilator vertically and surged upwards. "Topper, rocket thrust. Triple speed. Engaging power cells. Rocket thrust, NOW!"

The submarine vaulted up the manta ray's belly, cutting open a long slit. Out came thousands of pounds of human skeletons and debris from cars and buildings. The manta ray sank down into the ocean, bleeding out.

Everybody went wild.

What came next gave them nothing to celebrate.

Five sharks the size of The Statue of Liberty flanked The Annihilator. The sharks spun in a formation, causing the submarine to lose its bearing and flip. The enormous squid charging in added to the frenzy. Every one of its tentacle bashed the outside of The Annihilator. Each strike was a jolting punch that nearly sent everybody out of his or her seat. Anchor could only imagine what the poor cadets below the bridge were suffering.

"Fire what you got!" Anchor commanded. "Get these things off our ass!"

Olsen unleashed a wave of strobe flash missiles. The squid gave a roar that sounded like metal bending to incredible weight. The sharks crisscrossed paths, escaping the intense blinking light. One shark was swimming headfirst towards their sub.

"Double shields," Anchor shouted, thinking fast, "maximum speed! Ramming time!"

The Annihilator slammed right into the shark's face. The vessel's impact caused the shark's head to go up into highflying mist.

"*Whoooa-yeaaaaah!*" Anchor shouted. "Take that, fish bait. Hook 'em and cook 'em! I'm fucking hungry! Reel 'em in!"

"Olsen, fire out some more of those strobe flashes," Anchor ordered. "Maintain position. The flashes will buy us a few moments to recover our bearings."

Olsen released more strobe flashes.

When the flashes cleared, their situation wasn't any better.

It became astronomically worse.

Anchor could only take in the information on the screen image by image. The mega Beluga whale dominated the scene. The bulk was half-white skin and half bone with demon red eyes. Its teeth were the size of skyscrapers. Those teeth skewered the attack subs in its path and chewed them into pieces. Those pieces were swallowed in the deep gulf of a throat and spewed out the long row of blowholes at hundreds of miles an hour. Another whale, this one a mega Killer Whale, head butted subs and swatted its tail to explode the vessels. Two more manta rays, dozens of giant sharks, and a fleet of squid followed up the new line of sea creatures.

How many enemies had Gargantuan produced, Anchor wondered. Where had the other enemies come from moments ago?

Anchor knew the answer to that. He didn't need to be a marine biologist or of a scientific mind to know. This *was* an ambush. These monsters were waiting in the deeper depths to come together and take them out. These monsters were smart, as they were cunning and deadly. The Annihilator was in as much danger as before. The entire world could be crushed by this team of deep sea titans.

"That whale is playing baseball with our subs," Anchor growled. "There's gotta be another course of attack."

"There is, Anchor."

Dr. Singer had a 9mm trained to his head. The scientist had back up. Crew from below had firearms aimed at each of the crewmembers.

"This is my sub," Dr. Singer said, "and my orders are going to be carried out. Change of plans everybody. We're turning The Annihilator around and heading straight for Gargantuan. *I'm afraid I must insist.*"

# Enter Gargantuan

"Talk, I put a bullet through your head, Anchor. With the nozzle pressed up against the side of your head, you know I won't miss."

Anchor refused to be silent. Send a slug through his head. He didn't give a good Goddamn. This scientist could go shove a beaker up his ass, Anchor thought. This wasn't the proper way to carry out the mission.

"Where did they find you, man? You're not like any scientist I've heard of. You say you can steer The Annihilator. You snap a man's neck without batting an eye. Who are you really?"

"A scientist working on behalf of the United States of America. Now do as I say, or you each die. Do you want to save lives, or not?"

Anchor knew how to handle this before anything else needed to be said. He didn't want any guns being fired in the submarine. A bullet could damage equipment, and damaged equipment meant going up against the enemy carrying a gun without bullets. Crazy men with power, like Mendel and Singer, couldn't be taken on by normal terms. Man vs. man didn't apply here. Singer was psychotically determined to get his wish. When the time was right, Anchor knew when to turn the tables on the sucker.

"Okay," Anchor said, "we're changing course. Everybody, engage every weapon you got. We're entering Gargantuan. Do as he says. Resisting could cause more problems than helping. We tried doing the right thing. Now we have to do it their way. I don't like it. You don't like it. Fuck it."

"The guns stay trained on you and your crew," Singer said. "I'm taking no chances. Now, when you cross the energy field, if this sub touches one of those moving currents, we're cooked. The only way is to fire every missile we've got at the field and open up a temporary hole. Removing the missiles will also reduce our weight. We can drive faster."

"When a hole opens up," Anchor asked, "how long will it stay open?"

"It's difficult to say. Our field studies say seconds."

"Seconds?" Anchor sighed. "That leaves no room for error."

"This whole mission leaves no room for error," Singer yelled. "Now fire everything you got at her, NOW!"

Fragment torpedoes shredded through an eel the size of a subway car. Through its middle, human bodies trapped in clear eggs were crying out in horror as they were torn to pieces. Anchor swore that he saw for a split second, an old cadet buddy by the name of Mike Johnson, head fly by the sub's camera.

"Blast everything!" Anchor cried out. Seeing his old friend sent a thrill of rage up his spine and into his brain stem. "No more talk. Only killing!"

Anchor sent a zip line of torpedoes at the Beluga whale. His aim was the best in his class. He made a direct hit at its head. Both its tiny black beady eyes popped like splattered tomatoes. Bright followed up with a missile that when it met its target, the missile turned them into acid. The Beluga's face melted like wax. Down tipped the dangerous marine berg.

"Quit shooting them!" Dr. Singer said, striking Anchor across the back of the head. "Aim your missiles at the energy fields. Forget it. I can't control you, Anchor. You just do whatever the fuck you want whenever you want. We still need you, but not in that pilot seat. I'm taking over."

Anchor was hit hard enough over the head, he ended up sprawled out on the ground. He was paralyzed by pain. His vision was double. Dr. Singer was in the pilot's seat now. He was barking orders to fire at the energy fields flowing around Gargantuan. The electricity fields turned the missiles into large plumes of fizzy bubbles. When blue electricity met orange fire, everything turned a strange red. Through the red color, a small hole in the energy field formed.

Dr. Singer shouted, "Thrusts at maximum speed! Set your courses dead ahead!"

The Annihilator jerked forward at amazing speeds. Dodging flying, broken pieces of other submarines, and other sea beasts on the attack, they surged through the electricity field. Before Anchor could blink the line of blood out of his eyes, they were on the other side of the energy field.

The body of Gargantuan was even more hideous and disgusting up close. The insides of every fish, shark, and aquatic dweller compromised the sea meatball. Bones and tracks of articulations and vascular tissue pumped and throbbed with vigor.

Long, green, ropey threads that resembled plankton reached out to knock The Annihilator off course. At the end of those threads were hideous gnashing barracuda-like teeth.

Dr. Singer froze up. "Oh God no! We're out of ammunition. This can't be happening."

"Quit tying your dick into a noose to hang yourself with, you idiot," Anchor growled, getting up from the floor with raging pain coursing through his head. "You got us into this mess. I'll get you out of it. Olsen, use the strobes. Blind them!"

Olsen obeyed the commands. "Strobes fired!"

The plankton shoots vanished under the bright glowing flashes of red, white, and blue. When those colors were used, it meant the stock was empty.

They were in close enough proximity that they didn't need any more ammunition or strobes. Before Anchor could speak the next command, several officers restrained him.

"You did good, Anchor," Singer said. "Now let me do the rest. I know where we have to go to set those charges. We have to go in deep. The closer to the core, the better. Prepare for entry. Raise the shredders. Brace yourselves. We're going in!"

# Deep Sea Penetration

The front of the bridge's screen showcased the wide array of blades jutting out from the front of the submarine. The Annihilator had become a Suisse Army Knife. Anchor imagined staring into the inside of a super wood chipper of working precision blades from hell. The ones that reached out the farthest were designed to sheer and make deep cuts. A second set of blades extracted whatever was excised, and then the final backmost blades were spinning jagged toothed saw blades that turned that carved meat into pureed matter. Among the blades were thick plastic tubes that sucked up that pureed matter and shot it from each side of The Annihilator to clear a pathway.

The blades were raking, slicing, digging, spitting, and sucking out hundreds of pounds of meat every few seconds. The submarine was slowed down to minimum speed. Minutes into breaking into the walls of Gargantuan's exterior, the way was growing dark. Whatever light came from the hole that had entered, they were so deep that sliver of light could no longer be seen.

How deep would they shred before reaching their final destination? Anchor was getting antsy. He had his arms behind his back and two guns trained on him. These officers looked like the could shit their pants, or already had, and couldn't mask the humiliation they felt. It would be nothing to break free from their hold, clobber the group, and stomp Dr. Singer into the ground. That would be pointless now, unfortunately. They had to reach a stopping point before any retaliation, Anchor decided. For now, he had to wait.

"Projection Lights," Dr. Singer commanded. The scientist was tapping on the main pilot's console. "Calculating our depth as we speak. Hold tight and let the shredders do their job."

Once the two dome lights came on, Anchor and the rest of the crew were given a colorful view of chopped up sea debris. Tiny anemones, plated bodies, squid flesh, tentacles, nodules, mysterious guts that looked like pink, red, and purple seaweed, was butchered and liquefied. Anchor tried to wrap his eye around the strange details. Everything changed in a blink when they were suddenly in a dark tunnel. All around that tunnel were familiar things, though the recognition wasn't anything welcome.

A junkyard of broken cars, buildings, houses, and streets were stuck to the walls of the tunnel, among crushed bodies of partially devoured and mutilated human beings. The way the victims jutted up from the sides of the tunnel and swayed in the water, Anchor swore the dead were alive and reaching out for help.

The sub shook with the vibrations of a strange deep growl. The pilots struggled to keep The Annihilator on course as everything kept shifting due to the jarring emanations.

Anchor had to ask Singer, "Wait, what's that noise about? Where are we?"

Dr. Singer didn't waste a second to peer up away from the console's screen. He was too busy making calculations and figuring things out. He was annoyed to break his concentration. "We're in Gargantuan's lower bowels."

"What? We're driving up this creature's asshole? No wonder she's pissed!"

"We are right where we need to be," Dr. Singer said. "If we're going to set those charges, we have to be right in the middle of Gargantuan. If we're going to take her down, it starts with destroying the nucleus. Once she can't think or produce protein, everything else will collapse."

"You make it sound so easy," Anchor said, "but in order to set those charges, we have to park this thing and take it on foot. How is that going to work? Have we done all of this work just to fuck ourselves in our own ass?"

"No, most certainly not! We've planned this mission out meticulously."

"Why do I keep feeling out of the loop?"

"Because that's the way it has to be, Anchor. You've made it hard enough on us already. We have to keep you in line somehow, and that's the only way."

"So what if we can step out of this thing safely? Do you know what could be inside of Gargantuan?"

Dr. Singer took a moment to compose himself. "Once we find our position, I have no idea what we're going to be up against. That's why we brought you and your team here. We'll go in and set the charges throughout her core, then run back into the sub. You were the best man for the job, Anchor. You have to do what you do best, whether you're fully prepared or not."

"And what is it that I do best?"

"*Killing the enemy.*"

# Touching Down

The crew waited in anticipation for the next orders. Anchor could only feel his anger rise watching the masses of corpses lodged in the digestive cavity of the beast. So many had died. The pressure to succeed was on Anchor's shoulder. He refused to buckle to the weight, no matter what the cost.

Dr. Singer changed course. The blades chopped through a school bus and cut through the colon cavity itself. The walls changed to a brighter pink color. Fatty flesh and pustules were crammed together, bunched up tight. The shredders did their job, pulping what was in their way and spitting out the mess behind them.

Everybody gasped, seeing thousands of strange clear gel eggs scattered throughout the walls. The eggs were enormous. Anchor imagined them to be the size of a tank. Within the jelly oblong circles, were wretched black creatures that had no definition. Curled up fetuses that would become unstoppable killing machines.

"We're getting closer," Dr. Singer said eagerly. "This is her belly. Gargantuan can store these eggs for up to a hundred years before hatching them. She decides which ones are born, which ones hibernate, and which ones are aborted."

When Dr. Singer mentioned abortion, a row of eggs dissolved for no reason, fizzling down to greenish black tobacco spit puddles.

"I guess those eggs didn't make the cut," Anchor said. "Probably something that can't kick our ass, like giant sea monkeys."

Nobody enjoyed his joke.

Dr. Singer was steering them through the pink sack of eggs to the other side. A wall of stringy green flagellum brushed up against the submarine. Anchor envisioned a car wash.

That car wash turned against them.

The flagellum wrapped around the submarine. The shredder's blades were bent back until most of them were completely broken off the submarine. The sub was then thrown across the way. Anchor, along with everybody else, was launched from their position. Bright hit her head on the ground and blacked out. Olsen had slammed headfirst into the console across from him. Blood was streaming down his head. Topper and Wolfe were forced across the bridge. Anchor couldn't see where they ended up. Dr. Singer had taken a hard fall. The scientist clutched his ribs. A grimace of pain soured his face. The other officers were scattered on the floor, injured or shaken up.

Anchor grabbed the pilot's wheel. The flagellum was squeezing the submarine. The sound of whining and bending metal grated on his nerves. Any second, the pressure could cause the whole sub to break open.

Anchor couldn't power the steering wheel. The vessel was trapped. There was only one other option. He searched the system for anymore leftover weapons and prayed for anything to use against this stringy beast.

One acid missile remained.

Anchor delivered the pain.

The missile didn't go far before hitting a bone wall and erupting into a wall of flesh-eating mist. The flagellum was turned into smoking strings until they completely dissolved.

The submarine was released.

"What have you done?" Dr. Singer said from on his knees. The man was clutching his ribs. "Jesus, you're going to tear her wide open."

"That's the point, egghead!"

"We're going to go off course. Damn it, Anchor, use your head."

"I was saving our asses. You want this sub to be crushed? That was about to fucking happen. You wanna be toothpaste squeezed out of the tube? I sure don't."

"Brace yourselves, everybody!" Dr. Singer cried out. "Try to control the sub, Anchor."

Anchor gripped the steering wheel. The wheel was stuck.

"It's not working. We've lost control of the sub."

"Then we're as good as dead," Dr. Singer cried. "It's all over. I'll never get my samples."

"You'll never get *what*?"

The acid missile had eaten through the bone wall. Showers of neon green fluid sprayed from the ceiling out of oily orifices resembling showerheads. Pounded by the wave of green sledge, The Annihilator was coated in the mess. Green covered the screen at the head of the bridge. The submarine was dunked, battered around, spun out, and forced through the ever-widening hole in the bone wall.

Everybody did their best to brace themselves. Officers were thrown up to the ceiling and came back down broken-necked, skull shattered, or dead. Upside down, right side up, The Annihilator was punched by ever-increasing blasts of green fluids.

Anchor could see the screen on the bridge change. The green was leveling out. The Annihilator was being pushed forward by bulging purple tissue on the walls at increasing speeds. They were dropped from on high. Anchor couldn't see what was on the screen anymore. The camera had been shattered.

He braced himself to crash and burn.

They were all going to die.

# PART THREE: DIPLOMACY

# News Flash

Channel Eight News Rogue Report
Kristie Gaines Reporting from Behind the Lines of the California Disaster Zone

"This is Kristie Gaines reporting from Monterey Bay. I am here illegally. I have no affiliation with Channel Eight News anymore. I am reporting for the people. The Central Coast, along with the rest of the California Coastal line, has been evacuated. Behind me lays the ruined remains of cities and residential areas destroyed by the strange creatures reported to have come from the sea. As you can see, not everybody is gone. Looters are breaking into businesses and homes. The police are nowhere to be seen. Emergency forces are absent as well. The only crews around are the ones wearing Hazmat suits. These mysterious crews are collecting bodies and piling them into wheelbarrows. Is this disease control or a cover up? What we have is a failure of the government to protect their own people. Our coast and citizens remain unprotected. What does our military plan to do to stop this from happening again? Are we really safe from both the monsters and each other? We'll know in the days to come."

Kristie Gaines Off Camera

"Let's get the fuck out of here guys. Those gunshots keep getting closer, and I keep hearing noises from the ocean. I don't want to be around if those giant things come back. Did you see those dead bodies they were lugging in wheel barrels? *They were smashed to pieces.* Something is going on beyond what the government is telling us, and I'm going to find out what is really happening. I'll put my life on it!"

Captain Mendel in Person with President Ted Yearling
The Sub-basement of The White House
Enjoying drinks at President Yearling's Personal Bar

Captain Mendel's normal confidence had dried up during the past few hours. Ted Yearling, a three hundred pound man with bold white hair and a face the color of a burst capillary, was on his fifth bourbon on the rocks. Captain Mendel had barely sipped his bottle of oatmeal stout. The president stayed behind his bar counter, eying the numerous posters of scantily clad women. When female flesh failed to distract him, the president drilled darts into the board across the room.

"Okay, we've got some shit to clean up here," Ted grumbled. "I was afraid this mission had too much room for error."

"It's not over yet," Captain Mendel insisted. "We've lost communication, is all. One of them on board blocked my signal. That was intentional. Everything could be going just fine."

"Highly doubtful." Ted sucked on an ice cube, and then crushed it into pieces with his teeth. "Any signs of those creatures coming back out of the Pacific Ocean yet?"

"The last sighting was six hours ago," Mendel said. "Our fleets beneath the water have kept them busy."

"Did any of the attack subs survive the attack?"

"No."

"And no word from those on The Annihilator. Damn. This is looking bad."

Ted was drunk and highly reactive. He didn't like to lose. The man was a pork-bellied politician who thought America couldn't lose, right or wrong, weak or strong. Ted could spout jingoistic American propaganda and strong morals, while simultaneously butt-fucking an eighteen year old. Also, the soapbox had to be pretty big to carry the loaf's bulk of bullshit.

"Then we go nuclear," Ted said, raising his voice the way drunk people do. "We turn the ocean into a boiling pot until every creature rises up from the depths like fried batter."

"And poison our waters, as well as international waters?" Mendel shook his head. "No. We have to give our team a chance to complete their mission. The Annihilator hasn't been destroyed. There's still a chance they can blow her up from the inside."

"I don't like it," Ted growled. "I'm in charge. I'm the Executive in chief. I can shit in my own back yard as much as I please, and you, Captain, will clean it up."

"Listen to yourself. The pressure is getting to you. You should slow down on the drinking, sir."

"No, I'm thinking clearly, drinks or no drinks. It's called grace under pressure. I'm not cracking. I've had ideas for America for a very long time. Our economy is in the tank. My approval ratings are down the shitter. It's about time to unveil my plan for the new America."

Captain Mendel wasn't in the mood for this nonsense.

He was going to hear it anyway.

"You see, we hire some terrorists to blow up strategic locations in the United States. We keep casualty rates low as possible. When we use our nuclear weapons against these sea creatures, we'll blame it on the terrorists, saying it was the terrorists who muddied international waters. Everybody will want to see those terrorists destroyed. After our nuclear attacks, the monsters will be gone, no problem. Cinch. Two birds, one stone. This is the kicker. Then, we'll move Americans to a third world country as the nuclear shit in the air clears up. We'll modernize Africa, or Gambodia."

"Gambodia isn't a place, sir. Maybe you mean Cambodia?"

"Whatever, they're all poor and struggling just the same. Spin a globe and pick a place, who cares? We'll turn their country into a super America. We'll call it "Re-America." The white trash will call it R'merica. Yeah. R'merica. I like the way it sounds. It's like starting over again. There will be so many jobs created. Imagine it. We'll pull ourselves up from our shoestrings, get back to work, and return to the old values that made us such a wonderful country. Like pilgrims riding on the Oregon Trail. Manifest Destiny, new world style. We'll set sail like Christopher Columbus, but we won't rape the natives as his team did. When the nuclear cloud clears over the original United States, we can kick the natives the hell off the newly realized America. They'll go to the old America, you see. It's a perfect plan. Hell, a nuclear scorched America is a fuck of a lot better than how some of these impoverished countries have it now. It's humanitarian."

Captain Mendel noticed the small mirror on the bar top covered with white dust residue. Cocaine. The president was blasted out of his head. The white pony released the inner lunatic in the politician. Ted had as many hair-brained schemes as he had shit up his ass. That's why Captain Mendel advised men like Ted Yearling from making a big horse's ass out of themselves in public. Ted wouldn't be the first president with insane ideas, and he wouldn't be the last. Captain Mendel was here to censor and convince the president there were better ways to handle the situation.

*Re-America?*

*God help us.*

"Sir, slow down. You've got funny powder up your nose and a moonshine distillery cooking in your belly. Think. Really take a moment to consider what you're saying. Our mission hasn't failed. My job is to advise you, sir. I've helped you bury people under the system. I'm the one to help you make those critical choices when it comes to our nation's future. I have to be evil, underhanded, and maniacal, but also sound in my final process. When it comes to matters of national security, I know my business. Your business is people, President, and my business is diplomacy. I work behind the scenes, and you're the main attraction."

Ted liked what the captain was saying.

The dope still had one issue.

"What if your crew has failed in their mission? I need a back-up plan. You give me a back-up plan, I'll give your original plan more time to succeed."

Captain Mendel's cell phone rang. "Excuse me, sir."

Captain Mendel answered the call.

There was good news on the other end. Captain Mendel ended the conversation and returned to the president.

"Sir, it appears we're getting readings from The Annihilator. This is great news."

"I still want a Plan B."

"And you'll get one. Let me meet with my team. Give me an hour, sir. We'll come up with something good."

"Go to it, Captain."

"Sir?"

"Yes."

"You're going to have to go on live TV soon," Captain Mendel said. "You might want to slow down on the drinking and snorting. You've got a nation to address later today."

Ted laughed. "Reading a Teleprompter ain't shit. I've been blasted many times when addressing the nation. You do your job, I'll do mine. Now go on."

Captain Mendel
Sub-level of the White House
Think Tank Chamber
Emergency Meeting

Captain Mendel was ushered by a team of security to the think chamber on the fifth floor beneath The White House. He entered a conference room with six suited individuals. These people were members of a secret committee engaged in matters of covert national security. Hard decisions were made here, and Captain Mendel was familiar with these situations. These stern-faced deciders were only interested in one thing.

Gargantuan samples.

Only one of the suited individuals talked, and that was the silver-haired, hard-faced old man who had seen America in crisis dozens of times. Captain Mendel didn't even know the prude face's name.

"According to our readings on the ship, Dr. Singer is alive. He better perform to expectation. We pulled a lot of strings to remove Andrew Stevens from jail. We risk so much going along with your plan, Captain. We better get our reward. If Dr. Singer doesn't surface with samples from Gargantuan, your neck is in the noose.

"You've been allowed many freedoms with your position, Captain Mendel. You fail us when we need you the most, consider yourself dead. That could mean rotting in prison alone for the rest of your days. Or we could send you on a suicide mission. Maybe strap a bomb to your ass, throw you in a terrorist cave, and be done with you.  Better yet, we should let somebody falsely imprisoned have a shot at killing you.  Stick you in a locked room with somebody who has every right to murder you.  I'd like to see you in a fist fight, or maybe a knife fight.

"That's no matter.  You succeed, you carry on, Captain Mendel.  Otherwise, we will have to send a fleet of subs armed with nuclear weapons to put a stop to Gargantuan.  Our foreign relations with be down the crapper, but what can you do?  Our backs are against the wall.

"Our main objective is acquiring those samples.  Our scientists want live samples, not dead samples.  We want to grow more of whatever we find.  They can become a powerful weapon if contained, studied, and cultivated properly.  We can afford to lose American lives, but we can't lose this powerful biological weapon.  Stay sharp, Mendel, or it's your ass."

* * *

President Ted Yearling
Addressing the Nation

"My fellow Americans, I am initiating house arrest across the country for the next twelve to sixteen hours.  This curfew is intended to protect you against this highly unusual threat.  Lock your doors and stay in your basement.  Do not go outside.  Police and emergency crews will be checking the streets.  If you are out of your homes, you will be arrested.  We must band together during this vulnerable time for our nation.  We will succeed in our battle.  America does not back down to anything, human or monster."

# PART FOUR: CLOSE COMBAT

# Dr. Singer

Dr. Singer had banged his head against the pilot's console when The Annihilator made its crash landing into the unknown. He swayed in place about the bridge like a drunkard. He could feel the warm blood coursing down the side of his head turning ice cold. Crew members were spread out on the floor unconscious or collecting himself or herself. Every blinking light on the panels had gone dim. Red emergency lights had come on, bathing everything in that intense photographer's dark room color. Dr. Singer did his best to blink the double vision out of his eyes and move from the bridge.

He could feel the box vibrate in his pocket.

Captain Mendel was trying to contact him.

Dr. Singer managed to descend the stairs without falling forward headfirst. He snuck back into the conference room where he'd briefed Anchor and his crew on the mission. Deeper down in the submarine, he could hear officers rushing around to help each other out and access the damage done to themselves and the submarine.

Dr. Singer removed the box from his pocket. The box was a two-way communication device.

"I'm here, sir."

"What's the status of your mission?"

"Fucked, sir. I'm not sure if The Annihilator is functional."

"Have you set the charges?"

"We're inside Gargantuan. The ship crashed. I'll get the crew together and leave the ship to set the charges."

"And the samples?"

"I'll personally see to it, sir, that we get the samples. It's the only reason I agreed to this mission. I want to be the one to introduce this biological weapon. There's so many possibilities. I can't wait to get out there, and—"

"Put your chubby away and do your job. If you fail, I'll kill you myself. I'll be in touch."

"Wait! The Annihilator may not be functional. How do I get back to the surface?"

There was a long pause on the other line.

Captain Mendel was thinking.

"You're going to have to be smart handling this. Complete the mission. Gargantuan has to be destroyed. The samples must be salvaged. We're both in hot water if this fails. You have one option. You can only save yourself. Everybody else will be scraped. Once you've set the charges and acquired the samples, you go into the very bowels of the ship, and then you..."

# Anchor's Awake

"Anchor?  Anchor, wake up.  You have to wake up.  I can't do this alone."

Anchor opened one eye, and in rushed a massive headache.  His head hadn't stopped hurting ever since he woke up in this damn submarine.  The pain was only going to keep on coming.

Bright was kneeling over him, shaking him.  Her blonde hair was loose about her shoulders.  She had a bruise on her left eye, and her left nostril had been bleeding.  Everybody who survived the crash looked like hell.

"You're alive!  Thank God.  Topper and Wolfe are dead.  It's only you, me, and Olsen alive.  I can't find Dr. Singer.  He's not on the bridge."

"The rat bastard is up to something," Anchor said.  "It's a feeling I've had about him.  Ever since he killed Kipper, I knew it.  I don't think we're playing on the same team.  Better find the egg-brained fuck and go from there."

Bright helped Anchor up off the floor.  Anchor stopped in place seeing that Topper's head had been sent through his pilot's console.  Half his head was smashed into pulp.  Wolfe lay twisted up on the floor.  His neck was turned at a bad angle, snapped.  The crew, at gunpoint, had also ended up dead, suffering from massive head traumas.

Going down the stairs, Anchor and Bright removed themselves from the bridge.  Anchor could see Dr. Singer standing in the hallway.  He was clutching his head and regaining his breath.

"Dr. Singer, you made it?"  Anchor asked.  "What's your condition?"

"A bit rattled, but I'll be f—"

Anchor rammed his fist into the man's stomach. "That's for sticking a gun in my face and pistol whipping me. From now on, we work together, or we don't work at all."

Anchor squeezed Dr. Singer's neck with both hands.

Bright was startled. "No, Anchor, don't hurt him!"

"He just needs some understanding beat into him. I hate backstabbers. I don't trust you, Dr. Singer. Now what were you doing down here?"

Anchor let go of the man's throat.

"Looking for survivors," Dr. Singer said, gasping for air. "Calm down, Anchor. I'm only doing my job. Completing the mission is top priority. You were making things harder than they needed to be."

"Never leave my sight," Anchor said. "This is not negotiable."

"Fine, Anchor. Now we've got to find out who's alive on this sub and make a new plan. You going to help me or not?"

"After you," Anchor said, "but remember what I said. I'll kill you myself if you try anymore of that sneaky shit with me."

They moved to the bottom level of the submarine. Olsen was down there tending to the injured that were laid out on the floor. Other officers were running around, trying to access the damage to the ship fast, and perform damage control. After spending an hour with Bright, Singer, and Olsen bandaging the injured and putting the dead in body bags, they were able to return to the mission at hand.

Dr. Singer told the remaining crew, about fifty persons, to stay below, while Anchor and his team formed a plan to set the charges. They returned to the conference room. Dr. Singer stood at the head of the room and stated the situation in straightforward terms.

"The Annihilator is running on emergency power. I've talked to the crew, and they say the submarine is inoperable. We're running short on air, time, and power."

Olsen's eyes went wide. "So we're not going home?"

"Nobody is going home," Dr. Singer said. "This mission was full of risks. We've come this far. We must set those charges."

"And we will," Anchor said. "Put a tampon in it, Olsen. We're dead. Remember that when we go out there. Remember your loved ones, your families, and the entire world. They're depending on us. So let's get over this dying issue. Continue, Dr. Singer. How do we kill this thing?"

"Below, there's an elevator that will lower us out of the submarine safely, after depressurizing. We have suits to wear. They're lightweight and fairly comfortable. Down below, we have charges that will go off on timers, and there are specially equipped guns with multiple functions that we can use to defend ourselves against anything that gets in our way. Who knows, there might not be a damn thing that gets in our way."

"I'm not counting on it," Anchor said. "You saw how those muscular walls of that thing made us crash. It knows we're here, and it wants us dead."

Dr. Singer disagreed. "If it wanted us dead, it would've crushed us like a paper cup where we stand. A better guess, it wants to study us. If we don't set those charges and defend ourselves, consider your grave to be in a sea creature's test tube."

"No thanks," Anchor said. "So we strap on the suits you're talking about, set the charges, and then what?"

"We return to the ship," Dr. Singer said, "and enjoy what little of our life we have left. I believe there's enough bourbon in that cabinet across the room for everybody to enjoy. Then we say goodbye to this world."

Anchor could read it on Olsen's face. The pretty boy wanted to make good on the people he killed on that cruise liner when testing The Annihilator's capabilities. Now that he knew, he was going to die, all that virtuous crap went out the window. He regretted volunteering for the mission. Olsen's expression was cast in dismay.

Bright's face revealed something else. Accepting death wasn't something she could accept or deny, but she was ready to serve her country, and not because she was patriotic. It was because she didn't have any choice. That was Anchor's mentality. They would die no matter what. So what? They had a job to finish. What else were they going to do down here deep inside of a monster? Play cards?

Anchor had to say something to clear the air.

"If we're going to die, then so is this fish bitch. Let's get on with it. Olsen, you can cry into your pillow in hell. Now, can we get on with this shit?"

# Execute the Plan

The team stepped down into the bottommost section of the submarine. Here, the remaining crew stood outside the weapons supply room. One of the officers, a weapon's expert named Robb Fagan, delivered a crash course on how to operate the TAC-10 machine gun. Fagan was normally a handsome, well-groomed, mild mannered person. After having a gash opened up across his forehead, his life flash before his eyes, and survive only to learn he was going to die anyway, the officer had become a hardcore asshole.

"The last thing I ever wanted in life was to die seeing your ugly faces. I'm sure they have better looking trolls in hell. The very least you can do for me is listen to me teach you how to shoot this thing. Not that it's going to save your dumb ass if you don't have the good sense to use it properly. Judging by some of your freaked out faces, many of you are going to die before you squeeze off a single round."

"Shut the fuck up and tell us how to use the damn thing," Anchor said. "Enough with the bleeding heart shit. I bet you journal, too."

"Fuck you," Fagan grunted. "Fine. On with it. You see this machine gun in my hand?"

Anchor studied the TAC-10.

He imagined a chrome bazooka with its large barrel.

"The TAC-10 has several different settings for firing. You can single fire, auto-fire, or spatter fire, which means you can fire ten shots at once in short spats. If you see the switch on the side of the gun, you can go from shooting bullets, to spraying fire or acid. My favorite setting is the static-pulse. It's like lightning shooting out of your gun. Anything that light touches, gets their balls fried extra crispy. If you're in deep shit, and you're fatally wounded and slow to die, you turn that dial on the side to "10" and it will make the gun explode. That explosion can level a five-story building. Careful how you use it. I guess if you're dying anyway, you won't give a flying fuck about your ass. You see somebody go down, you might keep an eye on them to make sure they don't blow all of our asses away before we're ready to buy the farm."

Fagan reached into the small room behind him and handed out the team a TAC-10 weapon each.

"Don't be a pussy when you step out of The Annihilator. I can smell a pussy a mile away, and if you reek of vagina, I'll pop a round in your skull and cut my losses. No wimps."

Anchor wanted to put Fagan in a headlock and break the wise talker's neck. Who was he to judge these people like that? They were scared and in an insane situation. No training could prepare anybody for what was coming their way.

Fagan was just like the other hotheaded officers he'd met. They talked big to cover their own fear. Anchor made a mental bet that Fagan would be one of the first to die.

Everybody stepped into the other supply room next door to Fagan's room. The man was brought in special for the mission, known for his expertise in demolition. He had the face of experience and the voice of confidence. Paul Leeks introduced himself, and he had two items in his hands. They were black boxes that fit snugly in his hands.

"These are the charges you are going to be sticking up this bitch's asshole. You spread them out approximately three hundred yards apart. They'll stick to the fleshy walls inside Gargantuan by the hooks that will protract out the back. Once they're on, you hit the red button underneath the timer screen. This will arm the bomb. I will carry the device that will set off the bombs. The more charges we put out, the morel likely Gargantuan will float to the surface in pieces. Everybody take as many as you can carry. I recommend five per person. That is all I have for you people. Good luck. You have one last stop. Dr. Singer will advise you from here. We're America's best. Let's show 'em what that means. No American flag bullshit. Just flex those muscles. Do your job. Die with your chin up and your boot up somebody's ass."

The group was armed and equipped.  Anchor followed the group to the very last stop.  This was a chamber across from the weapons rooms.  Dr. Singer was in the front of a room with clear doors.  Suits hung up on the walls.  They were dark red with white oxygen packs on the back.  They weren't heavy looking like space suits or deep-sea diving suits.  These were made of state-of-the-art material; Kevlar meets silicon, meets plastics.  There was a plastic bubble over the head.  Something out of a cheesy science fiction story, Anchor thought.

Dr. Singer explained that much of the suit.  The rest: "We might not need the suits, depending on the atmosphere inside Gargantuan.  We haven't been able to determine the exact nature of the conditions inside Gargantuan. It's all been educated, scientific guesses."

"So we could all melt once we step outside?"  Olsen asked.  "It'd be a waste for all of us to die, just because of that."

"Wonderful observation," Fagan said, standing beside Dr. Singer.  "I guess you've volunteered to be the first to step out, huh?  Good, ole boy.  Any other concerns?"

Nobody said a word.

Singer continued.

"The suit is designed to protect you in multiple environments, atmospheres, and pressures.  If your suit is damaged, or cracked, you might, as Olsen put it, *melt*.  The key is to work fast.  Place the charges, get back to The Annihilator safely, and then we'll drink all the whiskey and bourbon tucked away on board.  It's been an honor working with our country's finest.  Now it's time to strap on your suits.  Let's get the job done."

# Going In

The crew was all business getting their suits strapped on. Anchor enjoyed the lightweight armor suit. What he didn't appreciate so much, was the claustrophobic feeling the bubble over his head created. It would slow him down in the field of battle, but what choice did he have, being inside a monster?

The room carrying the suits doubled as a de-pressurizing platform. It would lower them out of The Annihilator safely. The real risk was once they stepped out of the platform, what would happen? Would the pressure squash them? Or would they melt, like Olsen voiced earlier?

Everybody stood against the walls of the de-pressurizing platform nervously. The platform was a large clear box. Ice-cold air hissed from the ceiling from all points, blanketing them in a chilly fog. Lights glowed on the floor. There were arrows pointing to the center of the room. The center would drop down like an elevator and deliver them outside of the submarine.

Fagan's voice spoke into their headsets.

"Follow the arrows, Olsen. You're up first, kiddo. Tell us what's going on out there."

Anchor was surprised by his response.

"Yes, sir!"

Anchor could see the vague outline of Olsen move through the fog. The sound of the platform shifted and delivered Olsen down from the ship and into the beast. Seconds passed, and Dr. Singer spoke into the headset.

"How's it looking out there?"

"Holy cow. It's amazing. I've never seen anything like it."

"Are you alone out there?" Dr. Singer rephrased the question. "Do you feel okay? No pain or any changes of feeling at all?"

"No, I feel fine. Nobody's out here but me, and...funny looking walls. Wow. I mean, just, WOW."

Dr. Singer advised everybody to wait a few more minutes. Nobody spoke a word. The sound of cold air hissing was all they could hear. That, and Olsen going on about how crazy it was out there.

"Oh shit! What the fuck is that? They're coming! A horde of them. I'm going to cut them off at the pass. I need back up now. There are hundreds of them out there, and they're looking pissed off. I'm not alone out here anymore!"

A string of machine gun fire punctuated Olsen's war cry.

Anchor was ready for battle. "Get us off this thing. He needs our help!"

Anchor followed the arrows to the elevator that lowered them down. Four other crewmembers joined him. He briefly caught Bright and Fagan's face through the fog, along with two strangers.

Olsen was enjoying himself raising hell. "Goddamn, they're ugly! I'm not making them any prettier drilling them full of bullets! Join me in the killing. They go down like any other bad guys."

Anchor was ready to join him in the killing.

The clear box lowered down into a wide-open area. The Annihilator had crashed into a hill of meat the color of human tongues. The walls of the area were dark veal meat. Anchor imagined them to be in somebody's throat. This throat turned out to be a battlefield.

Anchor, Bright, Fagan, and the two other officers raced out of the clear elevator box once the main door opened. They raced forward, stepping on material that was soft and squished like mud, but didn't give like mud.

Olsen was up ahead, spitting machine gunfire in wide arcs. Up ahead, from various holes, cubbies, and hideaways, charged forth a horde of monsters. They were the size of SUVS. The beasts had pincer snappers like lobsters. The pincers were half the size of their body with massive crushing power. The sound of them clicking together was like heavy metal locusts. They were on all fours, the lobster-armed, crab-bodied enemies.

"Fallback, Olsen," Fagan shouted. "Join us behind you, I've got a plan."

Olsen was about to fall back when he stumbled. The man lost his gun. The lobster-crabs surrounded him. Pincers bit through his arms, his legs, and crunched through the plastic over his head and decapitated him. The second the pressurized suit was damaged, Olsen's body detonated, turning him into liquid.

"Fucking fuck!" Anchor growled. "Let that be a lesson. Don't let that happen to you!"

Fagan pointed his finger at his TAC-10. "Turn the dial to six. That's the Electro-Pulse. If we fire it in their direction at once, I think we can kill most of them and make them retreat. It'll sure shock the shit out of them."

Anchor, and everybody else, turned their dial to six.

"On my count," Fagan said. "Three, two—ONE!"

Anchor braced himself for a powerful kick. There was no kick. Out the tip of the giant barrel came forth a bundle of branches. Blue lightning. They spread out like active arteries, pumping electricity into the lobster-crabs. The room was blindingly bright with blue-white color. Once those branches touched the enemies, they were instantly electrocuted. They burst into sizzling chunks of high-speed seafood. Anchor dodged a flying pincher, and Bright ducked in time to avoid a clacking hybrid lobster mouth. The horde was popping and smoldering in boiling puddles of neon green ooze.

"That'll show 'em," Fagan said. "You always have to go up the ass first. There's no other way of attack."

Anchor laughed, "I bet you always go up the ass first, Fagan."

Fagan gave him a wild expression. "In any other situation, I'd kick your ass. Considering we're going to die and you still have a sense of humor, I'd buy you a beer."

Bright was stiff and nervous after the battle, but even she smiled. "I'd settle for ice cream and a foot rub."

The rest of the crew came down the depressurization chamber. While their numbers were growing, Anchor took a moment to notice the outside of The Annihilator. It was a miracle the submarine had made it this far. The sheering blades were twisted back and broken, while others were partially melted. The sides of the steel sub were warped, dented, and covered in dings and scratches made by unidentifiable enemies. A dome light from the front and sides cast the area in a dim yellowish light. The rest of the area was dark, except for the lights from the headpieces on their suits.

Dr. Singer and Leeks approached Fagan and Anchor.

Dr. Singer said to Fagan, "Let's break up into teams. We set the charges, and rendezvous back to The Annihilator in thirty minutes. I'll lead a team. Everybody else start organizing yourselves into groups."

Bright stood beside Anchor. "I'm staying with you. I don't trust these guys."

"Do you trust me?" Anchor asked. "Hours ago, you thought I murdered all those people on the cruise ship."

"I was misinformed," Bright said. "I'm sorry, Anchor. Please accept my apology."

"Done," Anchor said. "Fine, you're with me."

Anchor had eleven people in his group. Fagan, Leeks, and Singer had their groups organized as well. Dr. Singer pointed north. "Anchor, you go north. Fagan, go east, Leeks, west, and I'll go south. Try to stay in a straight line. If there's anything in your path, use the acid in your guns to burn through the walls. They're mostly flesh, gristle, muscle, and fat. Set the charges you have, and then report back to The Annihilator. If you come across any enemy resistance, you'll be on your own. Any questions?"

"Save some bourbon for me on that sub," Anchor said. "I'm ready. So is my group."

"Then let's complete the mission," Dr. Singer said. "Best of luck to all of you."

# North

Anchor led his team away from the submarine and the other teams. Down the fleshy corridor, there was a dark opening like the mouth of a cave. He set a charge at the mouth of the cave. Everybody else backed him up as he continued first into the dark recess. The lining of the walls were covered in long throbbing slits. He imagined the gills of a mega-sized fish. Beneath the slits, strange articulations and process pumped life into the vessel. The gills were glowing neon green, giving light to the otherwise pitch-black tunnel.

Bright was memorized by the transfixing colors. Anchor knew the sight was something they would never see again anywhere else, never mind the fact they were on a suicide mission. Liquid gel arms hung from the ceiling. At the end of each arm, was a cluster of fish eyes. Was this their security system?

Anchor trained his ears. He could only hear the running of fluids, the hiss of air from a great life support machine, and the dripping of water. Then Anchor overheard the squishing of steps.

"Hold back. Stay quiet."

At the end of the narrow corridor, he saw them pass by as a fleet of soldiers.

Fish soldiers.

They mimicked humans by their arms and legs, although they were covered in green amphibious skin. Their heads were giant fish heads with big beady eyes, and a red spongy brain was exposed on top of their head. Their hands were long crab claws.

"Fuck those things!"

One of the officers opened fire with a string of staccato bullet fire.

"Everybody take positions, damn it! You gave us away, you dumb ass." Anchor set his gun to automatic machine gun fire. "They're coming. No turning back. Shred 'em!"

The group unleashed a rip-roaring fuselage of bullets. Hundreds of bullets turned brains into flying steaming meat and covered bodies in plumes of green blood. The eight fish were in twitching pieces in seconds. Their bodies were so soft. Anchor stomped in one of their brains to make sure they were dead. Yellow mustard colored shit mushroomed from every broken orifice.

"Nasty," Anchor growled. "Keep moving everybody."

They entered the stretch where the fish men appeared. When all of the team was in place, the entrance sealed itself up. The opening melted at the edges, boiling like cheese, until the flesh sealed itself.

One of the officers tried to punch and rip through it with his arm, but his arm was stuck. The purple fleshy material was eating into his suit like acid.

"Oh God, help me!"

Anchor was about to try to pull him free when the tear in his suit occurred. Instantly, everything inside the suit exploded. The man was bloody slop.

Anchor took the man's two charges and placed them on the wall beside the opening.

"Let this be a lesson," Anchor said. "Don't play hero. Chances are, we're not going to make it back to the submarine. The goal is to set the charges. Nothing else."

"This place could be one giant trap," Bright said. "The opening didn't close randomly. It's like Gargantuan has a security system."

"As long as we blow her up, she can trap us all she wants," Anchor said. "Keep pushing on."

Anchor imagined them being inside of a purple artery. The walls were smooth tissue. Once they had been walking for five minutes, he told one of the officers to set another charge.

"Anchor, behind us!"

An officer pointed at the long trails of slime that dripped down from the ceiling. That slime hardened into something rock hard.

*Another barrier*, Anchor thought, *this is a trap.*

Twenty yards ahead, the narrow artery opened into a wide-open chamber. Bone hallways were covered in oily black secretions. The room stank of fish bait and decomposition. Sections of the wall were hollowed out to display sets of human torso bones. Mostly chest cavities, Anchor noticed, with the bones of the sternum shattered.

"Set three charges in this room," Anchor demanded, "before anything else shows up to fuck up our shit."

The ground started to pucker. Air pockets burst. The gel along the floor rippled with motion. The jagged notches of a spine, the red-plated shoulders and chests, the giant pincer on one arm, the giant club fist on the other, the maw of a barracuda, and the gleam of ten demented crab eyes on each face, the six-foot tall monsters rose up from the floor and stood among them in challenge.

"What are you waiting for?" Anchor barked. "They're not here to make peace. Shred 'em! Fish fry time!" Anchor waved his TAC-10 at the group of enemies. "I'VE GOT YOUR HUSH PUPPIES RIGHT HERE!"

Everybody followed Anchor's order.

The room became an instant bloodbath.

# Dr. Singer

Dr. Singer knew this was the spot where he'd get his samples. He lucked out finding a treasure trove of samples so soon. That meant he could sneak back to The Annihilator with little trouble. Ditching his team would be another matter. A plan was forming in his head, as the group kept trekking forward, deeper into Gargantuan.

The team had entered a corridor that resembled a giant sinus cavity. Random pockets of pustules and gristle-colored growths bubbled up from ceilings and the floor. Gargantuan was a mega-ton anomaly of function from the best of marine, fish, reptile, amphibian, and even human origin. Dr. Singer understood the need to exterminate Gargantuan, but her information, her potential, would be a shame to bury back under the ocean floor.

The bone walls opened up to a sort of courtyard. The word courtyard came to mind because the walls were now covered in golden fish scales. Tracks of smooth purple flesh created pathways around the green glowing garden. The "garden" was stocked full of plankton, anemones, and a strange patch that looked like thousands of clear gelatinous globes the size of softballs clustered together. Inside those globes were assortments of hatchling creatures. They looked like tadpole eggs, but Dr. Singer knew they weren't tadpoles.

"I'll set a few charges in this room," Dr. Singer said to his group. "Everybody keep going. I'll be right behind you."

The team continued past the sea garden.

Dr. Singer had a small pack over his shoulder. He removed a scalpel and sliced off three globes. He placed them inside a steel specimen container. He placed the gel globes inside, and then Dr. Singer cut flesh from the walls, took samples of the odd plankton, and carved even more meat from the walls with advanced circulatory processes. He cut out a bundle of clamshells that were like pulling teeth; the shells had long stringy roots holding them down into the ground. At the end of those roots were clusters of sea horse creatures.

Hybrid sea creatures, so strange, so magnificent, so bizarre, Dr. Singer was giddy viewing what he'd take back to Washington. He wished he could give Gargantuan a proper dissection. She probably owned a wild myriad of creatures and beautiful biology. He only needed living specimens. The rest of Gargantuan would be blown to pieces. He figured those pieces would float to the surface of the ocean, scorched. She would be dead by then, but her information was still useful. The living samples, though, would be worth much more to science. It would add zeroes to his bank account as well. Better, he wanted the honor of discovering new species. Dr. Singer would be credited for entering Gargantuan. He would be dubbed the bravest scientist in the world. Dr. Singer would be so famous. His impact on the scientific world would be incredible!

Dr. Singer placed his two charges in the room and backtracked. When he circled back through the sinus bone pathways, he noticed slime from the ceiling was coming down in thick globules. They hardened instantly, blocking re-entry or escape from behind him.

He chose the right time to make his retreat.

Dr. Singer carefully treaded the room where the floor was covered in fish guts. He wasn't sure if this was Gargantuan's dumping ground for her dead, or maybe the guts were re-used for food, or turned into new life altogether?

The scientist couldn't help himself.

He scooped up a handful of fish guts and saved the specimen.

God, he didn't want to leave so much unexplored.

*I'm out of time. You want to live on to carry on new research, you need to get a move on and cut your losses.*

There were so many losses to cut.

Dr. Singer hemmed and hawed; aggravated that he couldn't change the situation. He left the discarded gut heap chamber and hurried down several purple fleshed halls. Dr. Singer eventually worked his way back to The Annihilator.

His part of the mission was complete.

Dr. Singer had one more thing to do to ensure his safety out of the ocean.

Not even Anchor would find a way to survive this situation.

# Shred 'Em

The creatures earned the name Heart Rippers. Right when Anchor led the charge, one of the officers was grabbed by the fast-moving crab-thing and lifted up off his feet. That barracuda maw opened, chewing through the officer's suit, easily peeling back flesh, and bending and breaking sternum bone like twigs. A probing tongue worked out the heart, forcing the morsel into its mouth and eating the juicy hunk of meat it had worked so hard to obtain in two squishy bites. Once the officer was dead, the thing tossed him aside. The heart was all the damnable thing wanted. The corpse melted when it hit the floor.

"Jesus, they only eat the heart," Anchor growled. "If you're going to kill a man, at least eat the rest of him, you wasteful bastards! Waste not, want not—*WASTE YOU!*"

Anchor delivered a static pulse bullet at the creature's midsection. The branch of blue electricity split through his plated shell and boiled what was beneath. The electricity burnt the crab/lobster/fucked up monster until meat exploded everywhere.

Bright decapitated one of them with a burst of staccato bullet-fire. Other officers were hurtling hot bullets, pumping and drilling rounds until their TAC-10's went dry. Heart Rippers were shot to pieces, literally lifted up off the ground and landing on the ground in fluid consistencies. He thought they were making progress when Anchor's angle of the scene was tilted. He was knocked off his feet and tackled. Pincher arms had him pinned to the ground. The dozen beady crab eyes studied Anchor through his bubble. The mouth, that barracuda maw, was drooling rubber glue.

"You're not taking my heart, you fish fucker!"

The head went for his chest cavity. Anchor freed one of his arms and grabbed his TAC-10. He shoved the barrel into its mouth and blasted enough volts of electricity to send its head thirty feet into the air. Anchor kicked aside the rest of the body and stood up again.

Anchor switched to acid and sprayed the eight monsters trying to overtake him into boiling bisque. Anchor had to move out of the way to avoid the tide of sizzling acid-eaten stew.

Bright had knocked one to the ground and was pulling back its head with both hands. Once decapitated, she spiked it to the ground.

*Man, that's one tough bitch.*

*My kind of lady.*

Bright picked up her TAC-10. Anchor joined her in doing a clean sweep of the area. Only five of the team remained alive. The rest of the team had their chests ripped out and their bodies destroyed by the atmosphere. The sight of blood leaking out of the suits in heavy amounts was disconcerting.

"I'm not dying like that," Bright said. "I die on my own terms."

"*You'll die on my terms*," a voice in the headset berated them. "*Your lives were always in my hands. Don't think for one second I lost control of this mission. This is all falling into plan. You might be tough, but I'm smarter than you are. I'm smart enough to live, and you're dumb enough to die.*"

Anchor's blood pressure spiked.

Dr. Singer.

What was the bastard doing now?

Anchor reported back to Dr. Singer. "Where are you? Where's your team, Doc?"

Dr. Singer didn't respond.

Bright and the rest of his team voiced their confusion about Dr. Singer.

"We'll deal with him later," Anchor said. "For now, let's keep going. We can backtrack once all of our charges are set. Now, take the charges off the ones who didn't make it, set them here."

"Fagan," Anchor called out, changing the frequency of his headset, "are you out there? Report. Leeks? Report. Anybody out there? Singer's team? Report. REPORT, damn it!"

Bright grabbed his arm. "If they're alive, we can't help them. There's no way to know where they're at. We set our charges and get back to The Annihilator as planned. I'm getting awful thirsty for that bourbon."

"Okay," Anchor said, "but I'm going to see that son-of-a-bitch burn. *Somehow*."

The team searched for the next corridor to set their charges.

# Dr. Singer's Team

The walls were like a yellow esophagus. Fatty secretions burbled and boiled from the ceiling and dripped down the walls. Dr. Singer's team was wading ankle deep in sickening pudding-fat. Filters, holes in the floor, were processing the fat. Mixed in with the fat were human body parts, chunks of vehicles, a parking meter, a post office box, a dead goat, and thousands of things a mega-vacuum cleaner could've sucked up from the city of California. This was a processing center for the beast, Officer Harry Wade imagined.

Wade was panicked. He kept leading the team deeper into the esophagus recess. Dr. Singer was missing. The scientist wasn't answering on his side of the line. After the strange garden of sea things, Dr. Singer had vanished. Had the man been eaten by something? Sucked down through a throat and processed? It was very possible.

The six other team members were starting to notice the scientist's absence. The bigger problem, Wade didn't know the way back. They had walked through dozens of chambers, placing the charges throughout Gargantuan. There wasn't a clear-cut way back to the submarine.

Gargantuan was conspiring against them. Wade had seen entrances seal themselves up, like flesh curtains falling, or flesh boiling and soldering themselves shut.

"We're out of charges, Wade," Gregson said. "Can we go back to the submarine? This place is starting to get under my skin."

Wade didn't have the heart to tell them they were in serious trouble.

Dr. Singer did that job for him.

*"Maybe you're finally noticing that I'm not among you. Don't worry, team. I'm completely safe. Know your deaths will benefit science, and know that I'll take full credit for everything! They say scientists are all numbers, theories, and boring nonsense, but I'm creative too. I can tell the world how I fought so bravely. They'll make a movie about it, and I'll be the hero. I can say how you were scared, and I inspired you to complete the mission against the odds."*

Wade's stomach dropped.

He was too terrified to be outraged.

"You left us? But why? How could you at a time like this?"

*"I need living samples to bring back for military study. I can't bring back living samples if I'm dead. Once we blow Gargantuan to pieces, her remains will be damaged. Useful, but not as useful as living organisms. The Annihilator is out for the count. Alas, there's one safety pod on the submarine. Enough room for me, my samples, and the stories I'll share with the world. It was great knowing you fools. Someday, I'll see you in hell, but not before becoming a world renowned scientist first!"*

Wade was begging Dr. Singer to help them. Dr. Singer laughed at his words and then changed frequencies.

"We have to keep going," Wade said. "What choice do we have but to navigate our own way back to the submarine?"

The consensus was to keep moving.

Wade led the team. The fatty throat chamber was changing colors, from yellow, to neon red, neon green, to a dark black color. The throat opened to a wide area. Everything was leathery and black and covered in a layer of clear slime.

The way behind them bubbled up and sealed itself.

Gregson shoved his hand in the boiling mess, trying to force his way back through the other side. The mess dissolved his arm. His suit was compromised, and the bubble over Gregson's head was spattered in red. Wade even heard the uncouth pounding of both Gregson's eyeballs bouncing off the plastic.

*Goddamn.*

No time to let the impact of another death set in, Wade and the rest of the team were mesmerized by the formation in the middle of the room. He imagined a demon frog's head jutting out from the floor. The head was the size of a compact car. The eyes glowed a deep emerald green. The mouth opened. A deep bass moan sounded, echoing off the wet skin walls.

A large clear bubble formed at the frog's mouth. Once it reached enormous size, the bubble was released. The bubble floated in the air aimlessly. Then the bubble dropped, landing on top of Officer Grubaugh. Grubaugh was inside of the bubble and floating upwards. He pounded the walls of the bubble. What seemed harmless was now a prison. Grubaugh couldn't pound his way free.

"The walls, look at the walls!" Officer Calendar pointed. "This room, it's like we're standing in hell. We're all going to die. I didn't want to die being fish food!"

Up and down the walls, faces appeared through the black curtains of flesh. A guppy's mouth with golden eyes. A carp's callous face. The face on the underbelly of a starfish; two dots for eyes and a slit for a grin. A shark's gaping maw, filled with rows of daggers with insane chomping abilities. Other faces were folds of gills, bunched up tissue, and beady eyes circling masticating sea lips.

Each mouth could open three stories tall. The mouths opened and closed as if saying they wanted to be fed next. Grubaugh was helpless as the bubble floated to one corner of the room to the next. Gravity made the choice. A ravenous sea horse face received the floating bubble. Grubaugh's shouts for help were silenced when the mouth closed, and he was consumed instantly. Once the face had its fill, it gave a light orgasmic *mmmmmmmmmmm*.

The frog's mouth was spitting out bubbles at a rapid pace. Moans repeated, drowning out everybody's cries. Wade knew he was going to die, as did the rest of his team. Wade shot at the bubbles. Bullets pinged right off them. Electricity was absorbed. Acid evaporated. Their weapons were useless.

Two bubbles attached themselves to Wade. The rest of his team had already been forced into bubbles and consumed. Wade's legs were in one bubble, and his upper half, in the another. The bubbles were trying to separate. When they did, Wade didn't feel a thing. He was too busy in shock to realize he'd been cut in half.

Wade could only look into the mouth of the angel fish crossed with a lamprey, and soon realized what it felt like to be eaten alive.

# Boiling Hot

Anchor didn't waste a second leaving the chamber filled with fucked up displays of broken skeleton torsos. The team cleared the area and was trying to figure out the next direction to set more charges when Dr. Singer spoke to Anchor.

"*You're still alive, Anchor? I guess that's no surprise, knowing your fighting skills. You won't last. Once those charges are engaged, you'll be nothing more than bacteria lining the ocean floor. You'll be recycled into shit. I bet you thought you were tough the way you handled me earlier on The Annihilator?*

"*My team is dead, and Fagan and Leeks aren't answering on their line. You're all alone. You can beat me up, but I'm the one who's going to ultimately kill you, Anchor. I'm stronger than you are, I'm better than you are, and I'm going to make sure the world thinks you killed all those people on the submarine. I'll make up stories about how you tried to sabotage the mission, and how I, the scientist, overpowered your muscles and brawn to save the day. I'm going to escape in the only safety pod with my samples. I'm going to enjoy fame and riches. Hell, I'll even meet your wife, Anchor. I'll tell her lies about you. I'll console her in her moment of need. You might be stronger than me, you ape, you big dumb ox, you Neanderthal lookin', paramecium fuck, but I win! I'm going to brush my teeth with your dick, you loser!*"

Anchor's mercury almost burst from the top of his thermometer when Singer mentioned his wife. Then he busted up laughing. "You're going to, what?"

Bright couldn't help herself. "If he brushes his teeth with dicks, I'd hate to know how he flosses."

The rest of the team was rolling.

"*I mean, forget it! Fuck you! I'm escaping, and you're going up like the rest of Gargantuan. I'm the one who made it happen,*

*Anchor. I win. I don't care if you're laughing at me. Goddamn it."*

Anchor heard Singer click off the line.

"He'll get his," Anchor said, "no worries."

Everybody's morale spiked from high, right back down to low. They ducked into another fleshy pathway. This one had a bone floor. The walls were like the body of a jellyfish, bluish-purple and mesmerizing.

Dr. Singer had reported earlier entering a sort of garden full of sea creations. This was another such area. The creations here were much different. He imagined sea creatures creating a place where they could relax and enjoy a calming moment to themselves. This was a monster's serenity. A break from the stress. For humans, it was a morbid room from hell.

Giant clamshells opened to display fifty human heads. They twitched alive, calling out and screaming for help. They were alive! Anchor opened fire, breaking open the heads like soft pumpkins.

The room circled around them, closing in, as the sights of the room really sank in for the team. Intestines were stretched about the room. Bright blue light filtered through the walls of the viscera, showing tiny minnows and other tiny sea life swimming inside. Instead of seaweed growing on the rocks, human hair of various colors had grown out, giving the floor a strange texture. Hands grew out of a pile of plankton, the hands locked in a rigid position as if trying to break free from the throws of agony.

Anchor directed his team out of the room as quickly as possible. "We can't waste ammunition. Set some charges, and let's get the hell out of here."

The team went about their jobs.

Anchor put one of the charges near one of the hands. The hand clutched onto it, as if wishing for death. It startled Anchor. Everything had life in this room, even if they were disembodied.

*Thank God, we're blowing this place a new asshole.*

*Nobody deserves to live on like this.*

*These creatures are like fish Nazis.*

Going down deeper into Gargantuan, the way back sealed itself up, boiling up and hardening in seconds. Anchor didn't care.

He didn't plan on backtracking. There was no going back. Only forward.

Bright stopped. So did the rest of the team. "Do you hear that?"

Anchor trained his ears.

"It sounds like boiling," Bright said. "It's coming from below us."

Another officer said, "Does it feel hotter all of the sudden to you guys?"

The purple fleshy walls disintegrated all around them. It was like watching vinegar hit baking soda, how everything fizzed and turned to liquid. The ground vanished beneath them. The only thing remaining was a single bare bone, creating a bridge from one end of the corridor to the other. Anchor and Bright were able to keep themselves standing on that bone, while the rest of the team fell six stories down into a boiling pit of orange. Before those who fell touched down, their bodies were melted by the heat. Instantly vaporized.

Anchor noticed holes in the wall above them. Random items fell down into the pit, like other members of Fagan and Leek's team. The suited corpses were dead weight as they took the deadly plunge.

"It's like we're above the thing's stomach," Bright said. "That orange shit is its digestive juices."

Anchor set a charge on the bone.

"You out of charges?" Anchor asked Bright. "Because I'm out."

"I'm out too," Bright said. "So it looks like the only thing we can do is survive."

Anchor didn't agree.

"You're forgetting something, Bright. I've been locked up in a prison for a long time. I've been falsely accused of murder. My wife and family think I'm a killer. Let's just say I have some pent up stress to release."

"I don't understand," Bright said. "What does that have to do with our situation now?"

"Like I said, you're forgetting something. We're not out of bullets. I want to destroy some shit. It might be pointless, but it'll make me feel better."

Anchor released a blast of acid on the left wall. The fleshy material melted, giving Anchor and Bright an escape from the boiling belly beneath them. They made haste, escaping the hot box.

"So you want to shoot some shit?" Bright suggested. "Then let's have some fucking fun."

"Hell yeah," Anchor said. "I want to go out with guns blazing and my clips empty, and maybe we might fight Fagan and Leeks or The Annihilator. I'll ram my fists down Dr. Singer's throat so hard he'll shit claps."

Bright and Anchor clutched their weapons and took on whatever came their way next.

# Escape Pod

Dr. Singer was back on board The Annihilator. The lights inside the submarine were beginning to dim. The sub was losing power. Before long, the submarine would go dark. The vessel would be a useless hunk of steel. That's why his timing was so excellent. He was relieved to be out of his suit and heading to the escape pod. The escape pod was inside a key code room. Dr. Singer was the only one on board with the key code. The secret room was along the very bottom of the ship. A square of steel would open up, and the pod itself would eject. Like The Annihilator, the pod had blades that would slice up flesh, bone, and muscle. He would carve his way free out of Gargantuan.

The pod was a one-man submarine/aircraft. He could only lay in place and reach out to a control panel. Dr. Singer opened up the pod, placed the samples he'd acquired inside, and shut the entrance, sealing himself up in the pod.

Captain Mendel's voice spoke into his headset. "I've received the signal you've made it to the escape pod. You have the samples, correct?"

"Affirmative, sir. Everything's going according to plan."

"What's the status of the rest of the crew?"

"Few are alive, but most of them are dead. They'll all be dead soon enough. Those charges will blast everything to smithereens. It's a shame to strap a bomb to such compelling science." "You're lucky to come away with what you got," Captain Mendel said. "The media is breathing down our necks, saying we're not acting fast enough to ensure America's safety. The White House is bombarded with protesters. If they ever found out we hesitated this long just to get the samples, we'd have a real situation on our hands."

"You have ways of keeping secrets from the American public, sir," Dr. Singer said. "You do your job, I'll do mine. I'll be back very soon."

"We've got a tracking device on your escape pod," Captain Mendel said. "I'll have a team ready to pick you up. I'm on my way to the coast. I'm taking a private plane. Once those explosions go off, we're holding a press conference on shore to win back the confidence of America. I can't have you being seen."

"Understood, sir."

"Get home safely, Dr. Singer. This can't all be for nothing. All the lives lost. It's my ass too if you fail."

Captain Mendel ended the conversation.

The pressure was on to get home. Dr. Singer started up the submarine. All he had to do was set the controls to manual. The machine would find the quickest way to cut through Gargantuan and climb back up to the top of the ocean.

He imagined the awards, and the accolades and respect of his colleagues. Dr. Singer was too busy daydreaming about the future to notice his canisters with the samples. Still ignoring the samples, Dr. Singer took the time to contact Anchor one more time. He enjoyed taunting the bastard.

Little did he know, the samples would break free any moment.

# Stampede

"Watch yourself," Anchor said. "God knows what else this place has to throw at us."

That's all he had to say. The sounds made Anchor nervous. The incoming noises sounded like the pounding of many feet against puddles of mud.

"Where is that coming from?" Bright asked. "It's coming closer."

Along the fleshy floor, an ankle deep wave of water passed between their feet. Up ahead, they were coming in fast. Anchor unleashed every round from his TAC-10 until it went dry. It did nothing to stop them. Bright was blasting them, the army of angry sea horses that were eight feet tall a piece. They were riding the top of the water, moving at insane speeds.

"The bullets aren't stopping them," Bright said. "Shit, what do we do?"

"Spray the walls with acid. See if it opens up an escape route. If they get any closer, they're going to stampede right through us!"

Bright sprayed acid on the walls. The fatty tissues were bared back to bone.

"No go, Anchor!"

"Keep trying. Try through the water. The acid will cut through."

The raging sea horses were picking up speed. Their breathing sounded like charging bulls being strangled.

Bright emptied the gun of acid. The ground was boiling. Nothing seemed to be happening. Anchor braced himself for impact. Would he be killed instantly? He imagined them breaking every bone in his body. Instant death would be better than prolonged suffering.

The ground fizzled into nothing. Bright and Anchor fell through, landing in a fast-running stream of neon green. The two of them were being carried down so fast on a current, bashing against the leathery walls of the narrow recess. Anchor imagined them to being carried down a giant vein.

Through the neon green, Anchor could see fish heads rise above the surface. They were piranha in appearance. They had jagged spokes poking up from their backs. The spokes weren't natural to the fish. They were saw blades. The piranha bodies would vibrate, and then the saw blades would start spinning. Rotating so fast, the saw blades shot at them. It barely missed Anchor's head. Dozens of saw blades were coming their way. When they missed, they'd cut right through the walls.

Anchor had an idea.

"Bright! You hear me?"

Bright was almost cut by three blades at once. She dunked herself under the green and bobbed back up. "Yeah, what is it? You got some last words? I got some of my own. This fucking sucks!"

"Quick, grab my leg."

"Is that some sexual reference? You want me to grab your penis. Why don't you grab my vagina, dickhead?"

"Just do it. I got an idea. Do it!"

The piranha heads kept poking up from the surface. Once they spent their saw blades, the bodies would come undone and melt into the green muck. Anchor imagined them to be like bees once they used their stingers. Nature sure had one fucked up plan, Anchor thought.

Bright paddled hard and grabbed Anchor's leg.

"Now hold on. Wait for it."

"You better not be fucking with me."

Anchor waited. A saw blade missed, catching the wall. Anchor grabbed the tear in the fabric and pulled himself in. Bright was holding on, unleashing a thousand curses as new saw blades narrowly missed her.

Anchor used all of his strength to pull them out of the vein. Once he reached out for purchase, there was nothing to grab onto.

Anchor and Bright was pitched down into a long drop into the unknown.

# Pitch Black Walk

The fall was from up high, yet the landing was soft. Anchor thought he'd landed on fish eggs. There was no way to know what it was for sure. Both of the lights installed in their suits had stopped functioning. Bright had grabbed onto his arm. She wouldn't let go of him. The way was so dark. Anchor imagined glowing creatures suddenly appearing out of nowhere to attack them. Eggs hatching and killing them.

Anchor talked to avoid those thoughts.

"You okay?"

Bright sounded shaken. "Yeah. For how much longer, I don't know. That was good thinking back there."

"I'm going to get us out of here."

Anchor wasn't sure what made him say it. Maybe because he wanted to believe it. Bright called him out on it.

"I don't mean to squash your dreams or anything, but you're forgetting something. We're inside of a giant monster without a way out. You can't win every battle. We're not escaping. This is where we're going to die."

"I've been through too much to give up," Anchor argued. "I've lost too much in my life to have anything else be taken away. I'm not dying here."

"Yes, we are," Bright said, "but while we're here, we might as well keep moving. I don't want to die in some dark hole. We hold each other's arms and move forward. Sound like a plan?"

Anchor imagined his future. He couldn't create a picture in his mind, because Bright was right. This is the place where they would die.

"Fine. We keep moving."

A crackle came on the line.

"Not now," Anchor growled. "The last thing I want to hear is that son-of-a-bitch talk."

Dr. Singer spoke to them.

*"I thought I'd take the time out to say goodbye. I'm currently well on my way to safety. My escape pod is cutting through Gargantuan as we speak. I'm so close. Don't forget what I promised, Anchor. I'll tell the world how you murdered your fellow officers, and how you tried to kill me. You did so much to jeopardize the mission. I'll apologize on your behalf to America. I'll apologize to your ex-wife. I wonder if she's dating anyone?*

*"I'll tell her how it wasn't her fault you became the way you are, Anchor. I'll build her up and tell her how she deserves better. I'll be the one to give her better. With the amount of money and fame, I can have any woman. Just imagine what everybody who ever knew or loved you will think of you, Anchor, when I'm done telling my story."*

Bright was trying to tell him not to bother responding. They were helpless to change anything.

Anchor didn't care.

"You're not going to touch my ex-wife, you sick son-of-a-bitch. She's more woman than you can handle. She's a smart one. She'll sniff out a rotten bastard like yourself. Kill me, but don't go after my family."

*"Say what you want, call me what you want, but you're wasting your breath,"* Singer laughed. *"Everything's in my hands. You're a whipping boy, Anchor. Captain Mendel used you to take the fall for Olsen, and Olsen's dead now. Wow. You lost everything, in a nutshell, for no good reason. Your life was thrown away like a dirty diaper. Sometimes, the world has a way of flushing away its own shit. Nature works in mysterious ways. Well, so does humanity."*

"You're right," Anchor said. "You can say whatever you want. I can't stop you, but there's one thing I have to ask you. Are you still planning on brushing your teeth with my dick?"

Before Dr. Singer could reply, he let out a great shriek.

"No, what's happening? The samples. THE SAMPLES!"

The line cut out after Dr. Singer sounded off more terror.

"It sounded like he was being ripped apart," Bright said. "I never heard a person make such noises before, and I've heard some crazy shit today."

"It's all sweet music to my ears."

For the first time in a while, Anchor was starting to feel upbeat about the situation.

The two of them kept on walking in the darkness.

# Escape Pod Sabotage

There was something up his ass.

Damn it, there was something up his ass!

Dr. Singer unleashed the pain of having his lower regions invaded. Something tore through his suit and was having at it.

*No, no, no, no, this can't be happening!*

Hot blood was splashing the insides of the pod.

*"Whoa-nooooooooooo!"*

Empty sample containers were rolling in the pod.

Had everything he collected snuck up his ass?

Dr. Singer dialed up Captain Mendel's frequency. "The samples, listen to me, they're loose! You have to help me. The pain. Please. There has to be something you can do for me. *Ahhhhhhhhhhhh!"*

Dr. Singer screeched in torment. His abdomen cramped up with crawling things. His brains were expanding in his skull. Both his eyes popped out and were replaced by blossoming anemones. A slit down his stomach spread open. Frogs, jellyfish, eels, crawdads, shrimp, clams, and a collection of bacteria-eating sea life were shoving the guts out of his body. He was snorting thumb-tip sized starfish out of his nostrils. He shook his head, and slippery minnows splashed free from his ears. The flesh along his hands ripped, revealing pincers for hands.

Dr. Singer used those pincers to decapitate his own head.

Minutes later, the escape pod equipment was damaged by the infestation of sea life.

The pod crashed into a boiling pool of Gargantuan's stomach acid.

# Junk Heap

The darkness surrounding Anchor and Bright turned into muted neon green light. Anchor and Bright were walking towards a giant junk heap. The stack was comprised of refuse from humanity: concrete blocks, broken up vehicles, cabs, buses, parts of houses, and dead bodies sprawled out in terrible death poses. This wasn't the best place to spend their final moments.

"Hey, you guys made it to the party."

The weak voice called out to them from the outskirts of the towering junk pile. The man was sitting on a car seat. Fagan was clutching onto the detonator to the charges.

"You guys the only ones to survive?"

"Yeah," Anchor said, "and you?"

"I think we're it."

"Listen," Fagan said, "I barely made it this far with my life. We were surrounded by so many horrible monsters. Dr. Singer sold us out. Everything went to hell so fast. I was thrown so hard during the last battle, I broke my leg, and my midsection is crushed. I'm in so much pain. I can't take it any longer. I'm going to set off the charges. I'm giving you fifteen minutes. That's it, and then I complete the mission. End of the line."

Anchor could've given a speech to send himself off in style. The truth was, this was miserable. Being a martyr was bullshit. He wanted his life back before Olsen destroyed that cruise ship. That would never happen. Just like how he wouldn't survive this ordeal.

What he wasn't ready for was Bright giving him a hug.

"You're a good man, Anchor. Handsome, strong, and unstoppable."

"Except for this one time."

Bright smiled at him. "You can't win them all, Anchor, but know this, you're a genuine person. Die knowing someone sees you for your good qualities. It's too bad we can't take off our suits. Fifteen minutes is plenty of time to, you know?"

Anchor was going to say something clever when from all angles, hordes of enemies approached them.

"That's my queue," Fagan said, coughing up a mouthful of blood. "I'm raising this place. Fight or die, guys. I leave the choice up to you. You got fifteen minutes before you meet your maker. Let's pray heaven has some beer and pussy."

Fagan engaged the detonator. The timer started.

The life in Fagan's eyes went dim.

Fagan was dead.

They had fifteen minutes to live.

Anchor growled. "The next best thing after sex is kicking some ass! You with me?"

Anchor didn't have to wait for an answer.

Bright was one-step ahead of him.

"Look, this heap isn't all trash," Bright said, picking up a Winchester 1300 pump-action shotgun. "There are weapons scattered all over the place. Whatever those monsters sucked up from the cities, a lot of people did their best to fight back."

"A lot of good it did them," Anchor said. "May they rest in peace."

"This bitch will rest in pieces soon enough. This is revenge, Anchor. We're going to save so many people by what we've done today. This is a good thing."

"And meanwhile, men like Captain Mendel get to ruin lives and manipulate the government and its people. I've had enough of that shit. I'm stuck in the belly of this huge bitch, and there isn't a damn thing I can do about it. I'm going to die being labeled a mass murderer."

"No time, Anchor! They're coming."

Bright was correct.

She unloaded three thundering shots from the Winchester. The booms disembodied two of the Heart Rippers they'd encountered earlier. When Bright emptied the gun into more of the crab monsters, she dove and scooped up an M-16. The metal beast prattled fire, shredding into a giant school of flying fish with thorns pointing out of their heads and champing barracuda mouths. As the red meat fodder slapped the walls and floor, Anchor located a Mossberg 590 shotgun.

The Mossberg hit hard, delivering a lead fist into the face of what looked like a bear covered in threads of algae and gill slits going down its midsection. The algae creature landed in two pieces on the killing floor.

Churning out bullets, hurling curses, spraying, blasting, and pumping more and more burning hot lead, they watched a legion of sea horses go up into pureed pink.

"America will learn from this," Bright said. "It will point out the flaws in their government. They haven't handled this matter of national security with much grace."

"Nobody will know any better," Anchor growled back, picking up a Remington 870 and removing the severed human hand still clutching onto the stock. "The government will cover up everything. The people will be happy they are safe. The media will be manipulated to say what the government makes them say. It's the same I scratch your back, you scratch mine."

Anchor shoved the barrel into an incoming shark's face that had three tiers of teeth and at least twenty steely black eyes and pulled the trigger until the thing was decapitated.

"But in this case," Anchor continued, "it's, I'll scratch you back, you lick my balls! Fucking media, fucking government, fucking bullshit! Fuck everybody! But most of all, FUCK THESE FISH!"

Anchor used the Remington to cut the flying anaconda sized eel into three pieces before it could hurl itself across the battlefield and wrap itself around him. Bright had two Berettas and was pumping both at the hail of flying starfish that threatened to flank her from all corners. Anchor ducked, rolled, and used the last three shots from the Remington to turn the deadly starfish into stardust.

Puffer fish with gnarly pumping veins and sucker mouths were being shot out a giant wad of flesh with dorsal fins and lobster pinchers. Anchor imagined a tennis ball shoot shooting out tennis balls.

"They're bringing out the big guns," Anchor said. "They just keep getting uglier."

"Keep rearranging their faces," Bright said, spitting bloody scales off her lips. "Maybe something pretty will turn out."

Together, they said, "*Nah.*"

Bright was using a mini-Uzi to hold off the puffer fish. The puffers were small enough, one shot made them burst into nasty confetti. Each pop was like a leather balloon pricked with a sharp blade.

"That monster keeps launching puffer fish at us," Bright said. "I'm out of ammo."

"No problem," Anchor said, retrieving a M90 rocket launcher. The launcher was jammed into a rotten soft torso of a woman. He imagined a toothpick stuck into a club sandwich. "I got you covered."

Anchor brushed off a pale length of intestine from the barrel, set his sights on the crab meatball, and unleashed a rocket of fury. The meatball was lifted off its pinchers and pulled apart mid-air into burning pieces.

"Anchor, watch out!"

Out another shadowy tunnel, bubbles were flying into the room. Fleshy material shifted and stretched from the walls revealing fishy mouths and callous predator eyes. Hundreds of fish consisting of various colors, all armed with teeth and an insatiable hunger, kept charging after them. Anchor and Bright emptied two dozen of different guns at the incoming crowd.

"We're outnumbered," Bright said. Fear was creeping into her voice. "I think our time's up."

Anchor held her close. He knew in that moment, his previous life, his family and friends, were a thing of the past. They had left him behind because they were told lies. He couldn't change that. The only thing he could change was how he spent the rest of what so very little life he still had left to spend.

"If you're the last face I see alive, I think I can die a happy man."

"That's the sweetest thing someone's said to me in years," Bright said. "It really is too bad we can't take off our suits. We'd have some fun."

They embraced each other. Anchor appreciated the contact, despite their suits. The monsters were coming in for the attack. Death was imminent. The detonators had to be close to reaching the final seconds before the explosion.

Before anything else happened, the fleshy ground sucked them down. They were blanketed in walls of purple muscle tissue. Anchor couldn't see anything anymore. Everything was black. He could hear Bright calling out to him. There wasn't time to find her or do anything. The bombs were going off.

# PART FIVE: AFTERMATH

# Gargantuan Go Boom

Admiral Hardeman had a perfect view of Gargantuan when she exploded. Hardeman and his submarine crew had fought the deep sea creatures for hours. Gargantuan was like a giant meatball heated in a microwave for too long. Out the top, from all sides, walls of high-speed meat shot forth. Plumes of liquid flesh and ten different shades of blood, slime, and fish muck colored the ocean. Multiple explosions rocked the waters. The force of it knocked back the fleet of subs closest to the monster. After righting the vessel, Hardeman and his crew cheered in victory.

"Prepare missiles," Hardeman said to his elated crew. "We're not out of this yet. Those sea monsters surrounding Gargantuan are still alive."

Hardeman had misspoke.

"Hold on. Wait a second."

Hardeman watched the giant stingray, the mega turtle, and the rest of the monsters start to float to the surface. Their bodies were limp. Dead. It was as if when Gargantuan died, so did her spawn. Hardeman and his crew held their positions.

Anything could happen.

He didn't trust anything in the ocean anymore.

Pilot Reena Mitchell was hovering above the ocean near the Golden Gate Bridge. The fleet of National Guard helicopters eyed the waters for any activity. The water suddenly boiled with movement. Bursting forth to the surface, chunks of purple and yellow meat mixed with pockets of blubber and fat in thousand pound chunks. Tons and tons of raw materials muddied the waters. Military vehicles were stationed on the shores and along the Golden Gate Bridge with tanks and guns at the ready. Above in the sky, fighter jets kept performing fly bys in case whatever shot up to the surface was still alive.

Mitchell reported what she saw with pride. "GARGANTUAN IS DEAD!"

Reporter Kristie Gaines was laying low with her three-man film crew. They had been hiding out from the authorities to get their story. This project was looking more like a documentary rather than a news story. Kristie knew her crew was strung out and tired of eating out of cans and hiding out every time they heard military vehicles nearby. The coast was empty except for military presence that had tripled in the last fifteen minutes. They had footage of the sea kicking up nasty debris to the surface. They could smell it from their vantage point. She imagined raw fish mixed with battery acid and peanut oil. The stench stung nostrils. Even the gulls wanted nothing to do with the nasty hunks of debris that had beached on the San Francisco shore.

Now the area was really crawling with military on foot, up in the sky, and on the shore. Vessels were circling the mess. Boats were driving out, stirring up the remains, checking the depths for activity, and taking samples.

Kristie told her crew to keep rolling the film. This would be the story of their lives. What really bugged her was the way the government handled this affair. Millions were killed, and then the survivors weren't allowed to search for their missing loved ones. They were simply forced out of the city and relocated. Looters stayed behind and were committing crimes left and right. The true crime? Those looters were executed by the military. Kristie and her crew had footage of people lined up in the streets. They acted like a firing squad. This was really happening, she had to remind herself. This wasn't fabrication. Americans were killing Americans.

Kristie admitted only to herself how scared she was if they were caught by the military. They too would be executed. That's why they had to act with extreme caution and somehow still get the story.

More things were reaching the surface of the water. The collection of giant sea monsters that had attacked the California Coast and killed millions of civilians floated belly up.

The perimeter was cordoned off. Scientists would research the hell out of their findings.

Kristie would keep tabs on the activities.

This was the story of a lifetime and nobody was going to cheat her out of it.

# Public Briefing

Ted Yearling's Presidential Address
Live from the Beach Near the Blast Zone
Eight Hours Later 3 PM

Scientific crews worked in tandem with clean-up crews to salvage the remains of Gargantuan. Down the shore from this scene, a stage had been erected. President Ted Yearling stood proudly behind his podium with his chest puffed out and his chin held high. Select news teams were allowed to attend the briefing live. A Q&A would follow the address. Captain Mendel stood among the military ranks also attending the address. Throughout the city, military embargos were searching the streets, clearing rubble, and ensuring that the city was safe. It would soon be time to rebuild and repopulate the decimated California Coast.

Captain Mendel's thoughts were filled with victory and dollar signs rather than rebuilding. With Dr. Singer dead, Mendel thought, he was in line to be promoted and take Singer's portion of the credit. Anchor was also a loose end that had been tied. Nobody from that crew had survived to reveal how the military waited to take out Gargantuan to attempt to extract live samples from the beast. That part of the mission had failed. Millions of Americans died for nothing. Or so he thought until hours ago when scientist crews were reporting finding live creatures mixed up in the remains. Everything would be smoothed over, and he'd get his promotion. Captain Mendel was confident in his thinking as the president gave his address.

"My fellow Americans, our nation has survived one of its greatest crises. By the sheer courageousness and fearlessness of America's best, our naval forces have snuffed out the threat in the ocean. Our safety is America's number one concern. Soon, we will be busy reintroducing our citizens back into the cities along the coast. I ask volunteers to support in cleaning up the cities and helping citizens be reunited with their families. We will rebuild our coast after this untimely tragedy. That is my promise as your president. This is why America is the best country in the world. I am proud to be an American. I am—HOLY FUCKING SHIT! WHAT IS THAT?"

Mendel watched the president's eyes harden, and then widen in terror. He followed the president's mortified gaze and knew this situation was far from over. What was rising up from the ocean was...*unbelievable*.

# Pieces

Marine biologist Benny Simmons couldn't contain himself. He was bagging samples of Gargantuan, weighing chunks of blubber, and reeling at the crustaceans and aquatic life embedded in the remains of the giant beast. What would it look like under a microscope? How many millions of years of information would they gather from this fact-finding clean-up mission? Other scientists were working double time to hoist the remains by commercial net onto the large boat. What they had in the net this time was a giant chunk of fat. The crew was working hard to lift the chunk without breaking the equipment. When the chunk landed on the boat's floor, it broke into several pieces with a pudding's squish.

Dozens of biologists approached the sample with sample bags and dissecting tools in hand. Pus was oozing from the openings between the fat. Broken arteries were spraying green goo. They were ankle deep in mysterious blood.

Simmons reached in with both hands, submerging both hands up to the elbows. They had found actual live specimens mixed up in the fat. The fat and blubber acted as padding to preserve the creatures.

He latched onto something, and Simmons pulled it free. What he located wasn't what he expected. Simmons was punched in the gut.

"*Oaaaaaf!*"

Simmons doubled over from the powerful punch. The rest of the crew came to his side to help him. When everybody realized what had attacked Simmons, the crew helped the victim out of his suit.

"It's one of our own!" Simmons declared. "No wonder he came out swinging."

The man in the suit was disoriented. They gave him water and did everything to calm him down. The man kept saying the same things.

"Where's Bright? What happened to Bright? Did she make it? Help me look for her—we have to look for her!"

Simmons couldn't do anything to console the man. Their attention wasn't on the survivor much longer when out from the ocean came...

# Anchor Stevens vs. Gargantuan

Anchor couldn't make sense of the scientists hovering over him. They offered him water and asked him so many questions. He didn't care about anything they had to say. Only one thing mattered, and that was if Bright was alive. She was the only other survivor. She was also the only other one who knew the truth about his past. The second Captain Mendel found out he was alive, they were going to hunt him down. The same applied to Bright.

He had to find her.

If she was alive.

How could he find her? It might be impossible, he kept thinking.

Anchor was relieved to be out of the suit. He was breathing air, although tainted by the reek of Gargantuan's remains scattered about the water, it was still a step up from being in the confining suit.

The scientists on board kept asking him questions when the ocean shook with activity. Gargling noises, then the ocean bubbled and roared with movement. Anchor could see the largest chunk of floating meat. That meat imploded, something from within tearing itself free. Giant reptilian claws reached for the sky. Flinging pieces of meat large enough to smash into boats and sink them, Gargantuan proved itself to be alive. Gargantuan wasn't a big ball of meat. She was the monster hidden beneath so many walls of protection, and now that those walls of protection had been destroyed, Anchor knew this bitch was good and pissed off.

Flying up to the sky with its black leathery wings, Gargantuan was on the move. Anchor imagined a bone dragon covered in dark green algae. Fiery green eyes beheld the city below with callous determination to kill. The long plated lizard face screeched in the air, delivering a great plume of bright orange fire across the sky.

A declaration of war.

Gargantuan had the means to wage mass destruction. He could see between those notches of bone. Hidden were translucent sacks. Inside each sack carried sea creatures chomping at the bit to attack.

Anchor had to put a stop to the incoming destruction, somehow.

The scientists, and everybody in the area, were crying out in panic. Anchor couldn't save anybody by staying on the boat. He had to reach land and procure a military vehicle. Anchor could see tanks patrolling the streets. The skies were busy with jet fighters. Back on land was where he had to be.

Anchor noticed an unmanned jet ski floating on the water. He imagined the surging of waves when Gargantuan rose up from the ocean that had knocked the poor son of a bitch off his ride. Anchor took advantage of the situation, leaping off and paddling his arms fast. He climbed onto the jet ski and started it up. Seconds later, Anchor was speeding towards the shore.

He zipped across the water, dodging broken up ice burgs of fat and meat. Twisted sea creature bodies floated by, each one a gnarly combination of existing sea life. Anchor plowed through the corpses to reach land. Shells shattered and rank smelling meat made him gag. That made Anchor even more determined to reach land that much faster.

He ditched the jet ski and climbed across a stretch of broken up rocks. Above the hill, he noticed the stage. Members of the press were pointing up at the sky in terror. The military were getting into position and scrambling to prepare themselves for war. Tanks were lining the streets. Jeeps and military vehicles were circling around the president. Hundreds and hundreds of soldiers were occupying the area carrying rocket launchers.

*Now the Calvary shows up. Where the fuck were you when we needed you the most? We could've chopped this bitch up into even smaller pieces and none of this would've happened in the first place. Now you have you to deal with this flying bitch.*

President Ted Yearling was driven away in a private escort that sped from the scene. Captain Mendel had his own private vehicle. Mendel's eyes met with Anchors. At first, the captain didn't register that it was Anchor for several seconds. Denial weighed on his face, and then his features cringed with rage.

"Anchor! Of course you survived. We'll take care of that. I'm putting a kill order on you, YOU PAIN IN MY ASS!"

The captain spoke to several military officers, and then Captain Mendel retreated into his vehicle and fled the scene.

"Mendel! Come back here! Face me like a man. You stole everything that mattered in my life. Now it's about time I take something away from you!"

Anchor had to think fast. The car was a block ahead of him. He grabbed a big rock and launched it like a discuss. The rock almost fell short of hitting the vehicle at all. It bounced from the street and struck the back tire. The rock was jammed in the wheel well. The back tire popped, and the car spun out, it had been going so fast. It wrecked off-road into a mailbox.

"Score!"

Anchor was heading towards the wrecked vehicle to kick some righteous ass when a great plume of fire enveloped the stage. Gargantuan was on the attack! The reporters were roasted alive. Screams and cooked flesh put an exclamation on the beast's attack.

Rocket launchers were fired at the flying dragon beast. The blasts opened up the gel seal between its ribs and deployed creatures down onto the scene. Mutant rolling balls, mini gargantuans, produced bone spikes and plowed through soldiers. Human-sized carp fish with amphibious wings and foamy rabid mouths took flight, decapitating soldiers in split-seconds. Heart Rippers touched down, mutilating with sharp pincher hands, and tearing through sternum cages to steal juicy hearts.

The rolling meatball spikes were heading right for Anchor. He was unarmed, weak from battle fatigue, and without a clue as to how to fight this enemy. He was lucky to spot it in the corner of his eye. A motorcycle was tipped over on its side on the street. The keys were still in the ignition. Dried blood caked the console. The driver had to be dead.

Anchor mounted the motorcycle, turned on the ignition, and shot forward full-throttle. Ahead of him, another line of meatball creatures was speeding towards him. Anchor increased the speed, playing the deadliest game of chicken. Waiting for the right moment, punching harder, the motor heeded Anchor's demands. Surging on, he angled between two meatballs and avoided certain death.

The military was making short work of the meatballs. The enemies were on a smaller scale size. Bullets whipped them into shape. He watched rockets and machine gun fire chew and explode the creatures. Anchor slowed his motorcycle and stopped.

"Stop shooting your weapons at Gargantuan," Anchor shouted in frustration. Each shot opened up a sac on the monster's body and unleashed the monsters. "Cease fire!"

The line of military officers turned to see him. Their guns drew on him.

"Anchor Stevens, by order of the—"

*Fuck this shit.*

*I'm not dying for my country.*

*I'm living for my country.*

Anchor kicked up asphalt, getting some gone. Bullets pinged around the motorcycle, missing him by mere fractions of centimeters. When the firing stopped, Anchor half-turned to see sting rays wrap around the soldier's faces and squeeze, squeeze, squeeze, until their brains sprayed out of every orifice of their heads. The stingrays sucked up the gray matter and left the rest of the soldiers' bodies to rot.

Behind Anchor, a throng of military vehicles and soldiers were fighting back. They weren't ready for Gargantuan to unleash every monster under her rib. Coming down in the ultimate rain of evil, sharks crossed with crabs, fish crossed with eels, turtles met with flying abilities, every twisted concoction of sea life touched down and delivered war.

Anchor wasn't sure what to do. Should he turn around and fight, or—

No chance to think.

The decision was made for him.

Anchor didn't dare move an inch. Gargantuan lowered its head down. The bone face of the beast was only two hundred feet away from his position. The nostrils sniffed. Once it caught a whiff of Anchor, the face twisted up in angry recognition.

"You know it's me, don't you? What are you waiting for, come and get me!"

Anchor could smell the sulfur pits in its nostrils about to reignite and bathe him in fire. He didn't give her the chance. He revved up the motorcycle and sped right towards her face. Anchor drove up her face, missing the arcs of fire blasting from her nostrils. Driving across her head, he meant to guide the motorcycle off her body and make an escape. By the time he could, Gargantuan was a flying dragon in the air. Anchor had no choice but to keep driving down her spine.

He couldn't believe what was happening. He was so high up in the air on a monster's back. Any second, he could be knocked off and be sent plummeting to his death. Gravity worked against him. The motorcycle slipped. Anchor leaped off the seat before he joined the bike, which crashed down from skyscraper high.

Jet fighters were shooting missiles at the monster's body. Anchor couldn't stay clutched onto the monster's bone back for long. The concussion blasts of missiles, the way Gargantuan swung her body to fly, it kept jostling Anchor's hold. He had no choice but to let go and release himself to certain death.

# In A Bad Place

Anchor wasn't sure what happened between the moment he lost grip and hit the ground. He blinked to regain his sight. Anchor had landed hard on a set of concrete stairs. His right arm was broken. He knew his ribs were busted up too. Horrible pain rocked him into a paralysis. Under the sea, on land, everywhere was kicking his ass. He couldn't tell where he was for several moments. The area appeared under construction. Anchor's attention was quickly stolen by Gargantuan. She breathed fire at the jet fighters, turning them into highflying pyres of steel. Now that she wasn't being attacked for a moment, Gargantuan was coming back for Anchor.

What could he do now? He was too injured to run or fight back. When the military spotted him, they'd take him out under Captain Mendel's orders. Everybody was out to kill him. He didn't have a friend in the world. Everybody that knew the truth about Anchor was dead or on the wrong side. He might as well be dead.

Gargantuan was almost to his position. She was hissing and shooting out plumes of fire. She wanted to kill him so bad. She knew he was one of the crew that blew up her home in the ocean and killed her spawn. Sweet revenge was on this fish bitch's mind, and she was going to get it.

He was moments from being cooked alive where he lay on a set of incomplete stairs. Anchor couldn't help but speak his mind.

"You might've won this battle, but I'll fight you in the next life. I'm sure there's an ocean in hell."

Anchor steadied his breathing and tried to clear his mind and imagine his life as it had been once upon a time when things weren't soured by Captain Mendel's deception. There wasn't much time to imagine it, because Anchor realized something in that moment. This wasn't a construction zone. It was a demolition zone.

He heard a familiar voice nearby rage, "IT'S TIME TO DROP ANCHOR, BITCH!"

Bright was operating a crane and driving a wrecking ball right into Gargantuan's skull. When the wrecking ball made contract, it was a clean decapitation. The concussion was a thunder's strike. The headless body of Gargantuan tilted east and crash-landed into a collection of skyscrapers. He didn't have to see it to know she was dead. This horrible ordeal was finally over.

Bright ran to Anchor's position. She cradled him in her hands and told him how she washed up shore inside of a huge pocket of fish fat.

"Anchor, we're alive! Can you believe it? I mean, WE'RE ALIVE!"

Before Anchor could kiss her and share in the joy of living life, another problem presented itself. Captain Guy Mendel.

# Captain Mendel's Fury

"So nice to catch up with you two," Captain Mendel rasped. Crews of military were standing behind him with their M-16s raised. "You pulled off the impossible. You survived Gargantuan. *And* you've really gone out of your way to piss me off. Why can't you stay buried, Anchor? No witnesses, right? Nobody can know about what we tried to do below the ocean."

"Yeah, how you could've saved millions of peoples' lives instead of going on a scientific treasure hunt." Anchor stood up with the help of Bright. "How you arranged for me to go down for pretty boy Olsen's crime. I didn't kill anybody on that cruise ship. How many have you put away falsely?"

"As many as was required for national security's sake," Captain Mendel said. "The government can't run a clean ship when the bad guys out there are willing to play dirty. Sometimes, we have to muddy ourselves in the process of protecting the masses."

"And become a terrorist ourselves?" Anchor rolled up his sleeves. "You've lost sight of what doing the right thing means. Bright and I put ourselves on a suicide mission for our country, while you stayed safe above land pulling the strings. You've done nothing for your country but push papers."

Captain Mendel raised his pistol. "Enough talk. I can't have survivors telling the media what happened here. You're going to die."

Bright held onto Anchor. "All of this, and it's a bullet that kills us."

Anchor wanted to knock the gun out of the son-of-a-bitch's hands and throttle him. No chance. The M-16's would cut him down before he took a single step. Anchor couldn't outrun a bullet.

Captain Mendel gave him that mischievous smile. The one that said he had all the power the whole time. "Your wife remarried, Anchor. Your family disowned you. You have nothing to live for. I'm doing you a favor, and Bright, you're collateral damage. It's too bad I couldn't have spent more time with you. You got a set of tits that could make a man cry. I bet you would've given your life, and your body, to serve your country. In fact, maybe we can arrange something, if you're willing? I bet the president would like a piece of that nice ass too."

Bright unloaded a series of colorful expletives about Mendel's dick and a blender. Captain Mendel laughed at her rage. What he didn't laugh so hard at, was Anchor rolling on the ground, taking the pain of his wounded body, and coming right at Mendel in two seconds. Throwing back his fist with the propulsion of a sling shot from hell, Anchor's punch landed home. Breaking Mendel's nose, jaw, and his front teeth simultaneously, the captain was ejected backwards into his own men.

Mendel's words were a combo of blood and spit. "Execute them!"

Anchor knew the fury was coming. They would be mowed down. He didn't care. That punch made everything much better. Captain Mendel would remember Anchor for the rest of his days when he had to look at his new front teeth and how it felt when his jaw would get sore after eating something chewy. The bastard deserved a hell of a lot more.

Anchor held Bright just as he did when they were inside of Gargantuan.

This was the end.

Before the shots were fired, a series of smoke grenades were fired their way. Blinding white smoke filled the area. Anchor couldn't see anything. He drove Bright to the ground in case the squad starting firing blindly. Anchor was right. Bullets were being shot in all directions.

"Stay down," Anchor kept telling her, "it'll all be over soon."

When the smoke cleared, Anchor saw the bodies of Captain Mendel and his men chocked full of bullets and very dead. He didn't have a chance to access the rest of the scene. A gun was pointed at the back of his head. A hood was put over his head. He was forced up to his feet and carried off into a vehicle. He called after Bright, but she wasn't answering.

Anchor had no choice but to let his captors take him to wherever they were going to take him.

# All Over Again

Anchor was taken to a private room. This room had no windows. An iron door was the only way in or out. They had put him in cell. This was a deeper government prison. One where he would truly be forgotten. He had survived insurmountable odds to be locked up once again.

Whoever had put him in this captivity had set his arm in a sling. He had broken his arm. The rest of his body was sore. This was his future, he thought. A single room, all alone, waiting out the rest of his days to die. Anchor would save them the trouble. He wasn't going to grow old and soft in the brain in this place. He'd chew through his wrists and end it before the system could truly break him. Or would some other military asshole come along and offer him yet another opportunity to serve his country? What would be next? Rabid bears? Killer trees? Giant pandas?

He damned the system, damned his country, and damned his predicament. Anchor was so caught up in his mind he didn't hear the knocking at the door. When it opened, he was startled. Then surprised.

A younger woman with long auburn hair approached Anchor with caution. She introduced herself as Kristie Gaines. A reporter.

"I have been tracking your story, Anchor, ever since the first attack. I even recorded the conversation you had with Captain Mendel before the team took you here. I have uncovered a lot about President Ted Yearling and his treatment of the recent crisis. A lot of corruption has been revealed. The first thing that we've done, the state has dropped all charges against you, Anchor. You're a free man. I've printed the story. The nation knows you didn't commit murder. You saved our country. You're a hero."

Anchor heard what she said. It didn't have the full impact because of the man standing beside Kristie. His ex-wife's father.

"Can I have a word with Andrew?" Carl asked Kristie. "I think Anchor wants to talk to me. I'm sure you understand."

"Of course I do."

Kristie excused herself.

Carl approached Anchor slowly. The man was in his late sixties, but he seemed so much older now. He had seen the devastation during the recent crisis and was still making sense of it in his mind.

"I owe you an apology," Carl said, "and before you say anything, let me speak my mind. During the court hearing, I said some terrible things about you. So did my wife, and so did Angela. Just remember one thing, Andrew, we had misinformation. The government lied to us. Now, I know that does nothing to better your situation. I ask one thing of you. Believe in my sincerity. You are a good person, Anchor. Angela loved you with all of her heart. It's because Angela didn't want to believe the horrible lies we were force fed that she got so upset with you and moved on.

"If Angela was still alive, she would've apologized for everything. Angela died during the attacks. This crisis has taken so many loved ones from us. The California Coast is decimated. I don't have a daughter, and my wife, she's gone too. I...this is so hard, Anchor. I ask you to believe me when I say I'm sorry about how things went down. You can't change the past. You can only attempt to take on the present. Do something good, Anchor, against all this bad. Take them up on the offer they're going to give you. Make the wrongs right for the others still out there who are affected by our Goddamn corrupt government."

Carl shook Anchor's hand. The man wasn't much for hugs, even when Anchor was happily married to Angela. "Do the right thing, Anchor. Angela's watching over you."

Anchor was alone in the room to absorb Carl's words. He had so many questions and things he wanted to say to Carl. What good would any of it do? Angela was killed during the crisis. There was no justice in it. Angela died thinking he was a murderer.

*Damn everything*, he kept thinking. *Goddamn everything.*

Another knock on his door. A man entered dressed in a black suit. He introduced himself as Larry Beechum. Beechum was the former head of the F.B.I. and was now in charge of running a brand new government team.

"I work for N.A.C. It stands for New American Coalition. Kristie Gaines wasn't the only reporter to dig up startling facts about our nation's government and the handling of our national security. Outrage has spread throughout America. Citizens have stopped working and are picketing in the streets. The White House is a Goddamn circus. Americans demand reform and change, and N.A.C. is going to give it to them."

"So why are you here talking with me?"

Anchor wasn't in a sour mood. He was just sick of the government propositioning him jobs.

"You have become a national icon, Anchor. The people know of your valor. They know the truth about your false imprisonment. We want you to work with N.A.C. and clean up our government from top to bottom. We're treating the corrupt as traitors to our country. Those who've put innocent people away like you will pay. Our country is going to start over. We need the best of the best to pull this off. The incorruptible. You're it, Anchor. You're going to flush the shit out of Washington."

Bright entered the room. She was wearing a hospital gown and the biggest smile. "Let me talk to him. Anchor's been through a lot the past few days."

Beechum seemed to understand. When the door closed, Bright removed her gown. She was naked to the toes.

She crawled on top of his bed. "We can do this together, Anchor. This is starting over. We survived the impossible for a reason."

Bright kissed him the way a man needed to be kissed. Anchor couldn't keep his hands off her. "Together, we'll change the world."

Anchor was about to say many things and ask many questions. Bright put her finger to his lips. "*Shhhh.* Everything's going to work out. Now, would you quit worrying about everything and drop your big anchor inside of me already?"

Anchor kindly fulfilled Bright's request.

Everything was looking a hell of a lot better now, Anchor thought, while making love to Bright. Afterwards, he would accept the mission.

Anchor would be the one to flush the shit out of Washington.

# Epilogue

Machines everywhere. He couldn't make sense of the beeps and buzz sounds surrounding him. He was inside of a large room. It could've been a hospital, but he knew it wasn't. This was underground, or in the basement of a building. What was going on down here wasn't medically sound. Teams of doctors were rushing about the room carrying surgical instruments. Transplants and surgeries were happening left and right. The room stretched on. He couldn't see from one end to the next. What were these doctors doing to him? Steel and electrical circuits were being fused with human flesh. Pincers the size of Hummers were being grafted into big blocks of muscle tissue. Human lungs and gills were being combined. Digestive systems were enlarged and enhanced. Shark teeth and powerful shark jaws were being fashioned into new kinds of eating machines.

*Oh no.*

*Oh God no.*

*What is happening to me?*

They noticed him awake on the surgical slab. The doctors surrounded him, looking down at him with their giant fish eyes and pouty fish mouths. They were dressed in medical scrubs. Some had human hands, while others had lobster hands or pincers. To his horror, they could speak English.

"We've enhanced your body for the cause," the fish surgeon said. "You might've killed off Gargantuan. The battle isn't going to be won by force. It'll be won by cunning. It starts with you, sir. We'll do anything to conquer humanity. We saved your shot up body for a reason. One man must pay for what he did to Gargantuan. You will deliver that payback. Anchor shall die."

The patient could see his body in the mirror installed in the ceiling. He was a monstrosity with giant pincer arms, a shark body, and eight crab legs. He was the size of a tank.

Captain Mendel threw his head back and shouted in horror.

That ended when the fish surgeons swapped part of Mendel's brain out with a suckerfish's. Once that surgery was accomplished, Mendel's eyes turned red.

Captain Mendel growled, "Anchor shall die by my hands!"

The fish team cheered.

A new war was about to be waged against humanity.

# CHECK OUT OTHER GREAT
# DEEP SEA THRILLERS

## LAMPREYS
## by Alan Spencer

A secret government tactical team is sent to perform a clean sweep of a private research installation. Horrible atrocities lurk within the abandoned corridors. Mutated sea creatures with insane killing abilities are waiting to suck the blood and meat from their prey.

Unemployed college professor Conrad Garfield is forced to assist and is soon separated from the team. Alone and afraid, Conrad must use his wits to battle mutated lampreys, infected scientists and go head-to-head with the biggest monstrosity of all.

Can Conrad survive, or will the deadly monsters suck the very life from his body?

## DEEP DEVOTION
## by M.C. Norris

Rising from the depths, a mind-bending monster unleashes a wave of terror across the American heartland. Kate Browning, a Kansas City EMT confronts her paralyzing fear of water when she traces the source of a deadly parasitic affliction to the Gulf of Mexico. Cooperating with a marine biologist, she travels to Florida in an effort to save the life of one very special patient, but the source of the epidemic happens to be the nest of a terrifying monster, one that last rose from the depths to annihilate the lost continent of Atlantis.

Leviathan, destroyer, devoted lifemate and parent, the abomination is not going to take the extermination of its brood well.

 SEVERED**PRESS**

 facebook.com/severedpress
 twitter.com/severedpress

## CHECK OUT OTHER GREAT DEEP SEA THRILLERS

## MEGA
by Jake Bible

There is something in the deep. Something large. Something hungry. Something prehistoric.
And Team Grendel must find it, fight it, and kill it.
Kinsey Thorne, the first female US Navy SEAL candidate has hit rock bottom. Having washed out of the Navy, she turned to every drink and drug she could get her hands on. Until her father and cousins, all ex-Navy SEALS themselves, offer her a way back into the life: as part of a private, elite combat Team being put together to find and hunt down an impossible monster in the Indian Ocean. Kinsey has a second chance, but can she live through it?

## THE BLACK
by Paul E Cooley

Under 30,000 feet of water, the exploration rig Leaguer has discovered an oil field larger than Saudi Arabia, with oil so sweet and pure, nations would go to war for the rights to it. But as the team starts drilling exploration well after exploration well in their race to claim the sweet crude, a deep rumbling beneath the ocean floor shakes them all to their core. Something has been living in the oil and it's about to give birth to the greatest threat humanity has ever seen.

"The Black" is a techno/horror-thriller that puts the horror and action of movies such as Leviathan and The Thing right into readers' hands. Ocean exploration will never be the same."

# CHECK OUT OTHER GREAT
# KAIJU NOVELS

## MURDER WORLD | KAIJU DAWN
## by Jason Cordova
## & Eric S Brown

Captain Vincente Huerta and the crew of the Fancy have been hired to retrieve a valuable item from a downed research vessel at the edge of the enemy's space.
It was going to be an easy payday.
But what Captain Huerta and the men, women and alien under his command didn't know was that they were being sent to the most dangerous planet in the galaxy.
Something large, ancient and most assuredly evil resides on the planet of Gorgon IV. Something so terrifying that man could barely fathom it with his puny mind. Captain Huerta must use every trick in the book, and possibly write an entirely new one, if he wants to escape Murder World.

## KAIJU ARMAGEDDON
## by Eric S. Brown

The attacks began without warning. Civilian and Military vessels alike simply vanished upon the waves. Crypto-zoologist Jerry Bryson found himself swept up into the chaos as the world discovered that the legendary beasts known as Kaiju are very real. Armies of the great beasts arose from the oceans and burrowed their way free of the Earth to declare war upon mankind. Now Dr. Bryson may be the human race's last hope in stopping the Kaiju from bringing civilization to its knees.
This is not some far distant future. This is not some alien world. This is the Earth, here and now, as we know it today, faced with the greatest threat its ever known. The Kaiju Armageddon has begun.

www.ingramcontent.com/pod-product-compliance
Lightning Source LLC
Chambersburg PA
CBHW070337130626
46556CB00007B/2906